About the Author

Following the publication of his first novel, *Never Mind the Redcoats*, Paul Wojnicki quit his job to become a full time hypochondriac and part time writer. He has experimented with almost every single lotion, potion and snake oil that has ever been touted as a cure for baldness, ranging from eye watering onion juice to the breast enhancing sex change drug Spironolactone.

He remains, regrettably, hairless.

To Keith

No Cure for Baldness?

Paul Wojnicki

'I am not the archetypal leading man. This is mainly for one reason: as you may have noticed, I have no hair.'
Patrick Stewart

In loving memory of Bronislaw Wojnicki: Father, grandfather, great grandfather and baldy.
Rest in peace granddad.

Bronislaw Wojnicki 1926-2002

This book, including the section about the author, is entirely fictional. Any resemblance to persons alive or dead is purely coincidental.

Copyright © Paul Wojnicki, 2008.

ISBN 1434841782

Cover design by Paul Cook
All rights reserved. No part of this publication may be reproduced without the prior permission of the copyright owner.

Chapter 1

It was a shock finding out, to say the least. I'd had no idea, no idea at all. I think it was Phil that pointed it out first. Perhaps he didn't find it too rude because he didn't have a single hair on his head. I'll never forget his words, they will haunt me forever.

'You're gonna go,' he said.
'Go what?'
'Bald!!!'
The word hit me like a boxer on angel dust.
Bald.
'What makes you say that?' I asked.
'The fact that, from behind, you are starting to resemble Cadfael.' He wasn't gonna pull the punches then. I looked at him; the sneering cretin was enjoying this.
'Bullshit,' I scoffed.
'Fair enough, don't believe me then. But mark my words mate, you'll go.'
'Fuck off.'
Within minutes I was in the bathroom, trying desperately to align the vanity mirror I had just borrowed from Alison with the one on the wall to view the back of my head.
'Oh, Christ!' I screamed as I caught a glimpse of a sizable patch of skin at the top of my vertex. My heart leapt and my hands suddenly felt wet through. I dried them against my trouser leg and aligned the mirrors again. Jesus the patch was like a giant fucking crop circle carved into my once luxurious locks.
'You found it then?' I heard Phil's voice coming from outside the bathroom, accompanied by the sound of a number of people sniggering.
'Found what?'

'Whatever it was you borrowed Alison's vanity mirror for.'

Bitch. I'd asked her to keep it quiet.

'Look it's not to check for a bald patch OK.'

'What you checking for then? Haemorrhoids?'

'Haemorrhoids?'

'Well we all know there's a mirror already in that bathroom, so why else would you need a vanity mirror?'

'I prefer the vanity mirror.'

'Well don't freak out when you see the size of your haemorrhoids, those mirrors make things look larger than they really are.'

Of course, the mirror was concave. The patch might not be so big after all. It might even be my crown, magnified by the mirror.

That must have been the longest day I ever spent at the office. I was desperate to get home, anxious to examine the true extent of my disfigurement. That twat Phil wasn't helping either, whistling the *Kojak* theme at his desk, while Alison attempted to stifle her giggles.

At five o' clock I grabbed my stuff together, made my excuses for forsaking the after work drinks, jumped in the car and floored the thing all the way home. Once there I dumped my briefcase in the hall and made a beeline for the bathroom.

Confirmation.

There it was, a pronounced ring almost as large as it had looked in the concave mirror. A great big bloody bald patch. How in the name of punctured Jesus had I not seen this before? It wasn't like I was a stranger to the mirror. The depth of my vanity was oceanic, twenty thousand leagues, off the sonar.

I did not take this revelation well; I didn't take it well at all. I wept, smashed the mirror, punched the bathroom wall, grabbed another mirror, to get a third opinion and wept some more. I would probably have torn at my hair too had that not been the problem in the first place.

I was beginning to hyperventilate and could feel the tell tale signs of a panic attack coming on, the sweaty palms, the racing heartbeat and the tunnel vision. If I didn't calm myself down quickly I'd have a full on attack of the heebie jeebies. Only one thing for it; a cold shower. That usually helped combat the dreaded panic attack.

The cold water felt good, invigorating, like a difibrillator to a heart attack victim, CLEAR! When I was certain I had warded away the anxiety attack I grabbed my rather dirty looking towel from the radiator and began to dry myself, starting with my hair. I put one foot onto the side of the bath to help me dry the underside of my thighs and as I did so I looked into the bath tub.

The scene of devastation in that bathtub was as horrific to me as a motorway pile up. Shedded hair littered the bottom of the tub, dozens of them, fallen comrades strewn across the Perspex. Christ, was that normal? I had noticed hairs in the bath before but never that many. I began to count them, eighty four in total. Were they all from this latest shower? Or had some been there before? When had I last cleaned that tub? Two or three days ago, probably, and I hadn't showered yesterday.

That meant they were freshly shed.

'I'm malting, maaaalting.' I screamed as I sank to my knees, sobbing and banging my fists against the bathroom floor.

...

Sleep had finally been induced with copious amounts of Jim Beam, but it was fitful with all manner of terrifying dreams. There was no way on earth I was going into work today.

'Hello Neighbourhoods and Housing, Derek speaking,' my colleague answered eventually.

'Hi Derek, it's Paul.'

'Hi Paul, what's the matter? Are you running late?'

'No Derek, I'm phoning in sick.'

'Oh, OK. What's wrong with you?'

'Baldness.'

'Sorry?'

'Baldness. Hair loss.'

'Are you serious?'

'Of course I'm fucking serious.'

'Baldness isn't an illness.'

'Isn't it? Well it fucking well should be.'

'Why?'

'Why? Are you bald Derek?'

'No.'

'Then presumably you have never been bald.'

'No.'

'Then don't tell me what baldness is or isn't. You wouldn't possibly understand.'

'Well I'm sorry about your loss but I can't possibly put down baldness as the reason for your absence. I'll have to go grab a supervisor.'

'Look here Derek, I'm not hanging on this phone, while you try to get one of those bastards to lecture me on what is and isn't an illness. Just put my reason down as panic attacks, I have a long history. If there's a problem, tell them I'll have a doctor's note in by Thursday.'

'Well, OK if that's what you want.'

'It's what I want Derek, it's exactly what I want. Goodbye.'

Thank God I worked for the council. With my sickness record it was the only job that could possibly keep me from homelessness. I could be off work for up to six months at a time, on full pay and with my nerves I often was. Thankfully the doctor was always quick enough to write me a note, anything to get me out his surgery sharpish.

My next phone call was to the doctor's, I didn't feel like visiting the sceptical old bastard but it had to be done, in order to keep getting paid. It took a while for the woman on the other end of the telephone to find my name on the register but when she did she booked me in at eleven o' clock that morning. 'Yes it is an emergency,' I had told her.

It was nine fifteen now, I had almost two hours before the appointment. I might as well take a trip into town, buy some essential items like a baseball cap and a tanning lamp. Why a tanning lamp? I'll tell you why, because the first thing I noticed about the creeping flesh that was my monk patch is that its milky white colour contrasted sharply with the auburn hair that it was encroaching upon. Light was positively shimmering off it. A few hours under a tanning lamp might just take the shine off the fucker.

...

I was in town by nine forty and had bought myself a selection of designer trucker caps from an upmarket sports store by ten. I then turned my attention towards finding a suitable electrical store for my tanning lamp. Currys seemed like a good bet.

'Hi, I'm looking for a small tanning lamp for my girlfriend,' I told the spotty looking teenage shop assistant, when I got there.

He led me to an assortment of facial lamps in the corner of the shop and I picked up the cheapest one.

'Can I just remind you that it is important to read the safety instructions on this item before using it,' the pimply little bastard patronised me as we conducted the transaction at the counter.

'Yeah will do pal. You could do with using one of these things yourself you know, it might clear up those zits.'

'Sun lamps are bad for the skin.'

'Bad for the skin! Jesus how much worse could your skin get?'

'I don't have to take this abuse you know. I can refuse to serve you.'

'Alright, calm down pal,' I said waiting for him to hand over my lamp.

'There you go,' the oily bastard sneered, handing me my lamp. 'One tanning lamp for your girlfriend. Cheapest one in the shop. A real big spender.'

'You like big spenders do you mate? Well here's a fiver tip. Go buy yourself some Clearasil.'

'Keep it. You can put it towards a toupee, you bald bastard.'

'Why you cheeky little fucker. I could have your job for that.'

'Touch a nerve did I?' he taunted. 'My spots will go away in a couple of years but your hair's never coming back, is it?'

Each insult tore another strip from my emasculated ego. Who would have known that this skinny rat was the Mike Tyson of insults, raining in blow after vicious blow. I almost ran out of the shop as he continued to heckle me mercilessly.

When I was safely outside I ripped the labels off one of the trucker caps and plonked it upon my thinning mane, then looked at my watch. It was ten fifty, almost time to visit the doc.

Chapter 2

'Mr Hisky, what seems to be the problem this time?' Doctor Collins sighed as I entered his surgery.

I could hear the weariness in his voice, the old bastard didn't like me one bit.

'I've been getting the panic attacks again.'

'Have you been drinking heavily?'

'Well no more heavily than usual.'

'Been taking any drugs or medication?'

'No.'

'Exercising regularly?'

'Not really, I occasionally play badminton.'

'Well we've been through this before. The key to beating anxiety is cutting out caffeine and alcohol and taking regular exercise. I could give you more tranquillisers but let's not forget how dependent you got on them before.'

'Look it's nothing to do with lack of exercise or too much booze; I haven't had an attack in months until yesterday.'

'And what do you think brought this on?'

'This!' I shouted removing the cap.

'What?'

'My hair.'

'What about it?'

'What about it? It's bloody falling out that's what.'

'Mr Hisky, you are twenty eight years old. It's perfectly normal to begin thinning a little at your age.'

'This isn't a little. I counted eighty four hairs in the bathtub last night. My plughole had more hair in it than Brian May's.'

'It's perfectly normal for hairs to shed, that's what hair does once it's ended its growing phase.'

'Don't give me any of this phase bollocks. You're bald, what do you know about combating baldness? Are those adverts you see in the magazines true? How about those laser combs?'

'Mr Hisky,' the doctor sighed. 'Believe me when I tell you that the best thing to do about hair loss is to just accept it. Shave your hair short if you want it to be less noticeable.'

'Doctor Collins, I am six feet tall and I weigh ten stones wet through, do you really think I could pull off a shaved head? Give me a diaper and some glasses and I would look like bloody Gandhi for crying out loud. Shaving my head is not an option.'

'Well there is certainly nothing available on the NHS.'

'Fine, I'll pay. Just tell me what my options are.'

'Well I am aware of one topical drug called Minoxidil, it sells under the name of Regaine in the UK. You could look it up on the internet I suppose. Also there is another drug that is taken orally called Propecia, but with the possibility of side effects and your history of hypochondria I certainly wouldn't recommend that. Better to start on the Regaine and see how you go from there.'

'Thanks doctor.'

'OK, anything else I can help you with?'

'I just need a sick note for work, oh and could you just take a look at this lump I think I found on my back.'

...

I hate the smell of the library in the morning. The smell, you know, that all pervading sickly stench of stale sweat that down and outs exude. The whole library. It smelled like- poverty. Yes, I hated this place, but the internet *was* free to use here, which probably explained the reason it was so full.

Thank God I live in the age of the internet, that amazing wonder of technology that allows you to purchase drugs from faraway places like China and India for a fraction of the cost the robbing bastards charge over here. I only wish I had it at home, that way I could avoid places like the municipal library. Christ I bet the sweat shop that was producing these tablets in Mumbai smelled better than this fucking library. But this was an emergency, so I signed in at the desk and secured myself a terminal. I then positioned myself at my machine and entered the access code assigned to my library card. My first search was for Minoxidil of which there were one million five hundred thousand and seventy results. Google also suggested I look under 'Minoxidil side effects' and, being the paranoiac I am, I did so and got another four hundred thousand results. I clicked on the top link and began to read the list of potential side effects that might result from me rubbing this shit into my scalp:

Extremely rare side effects that may occur if too much topically or orally administered Minoxidil is being absorbed in the body include:

- *changes in vision, most commonly blurred vision*
- *chest pain*
- *very low blood pressure*
- *decreased sexual desire*
- *fast or irregular heartbeat*
- *flushing of the skin*
- *headache*
- *light-headedness*
- *numbness or tingling in the hands, feet, or face*
- *partial, or complete, impotence*
- *rapid weight gain*
- *swelling of the hands, feet, lower legs, or face*

I've never been able to understand why it is that side effects always have to be negative? Where's the drug that accidentally enlarge your penis while curing your stomach ache? Or the ones that enable you to fuck all night without coming too quickly? No, it always has to be impotence or decreased sexual desire doesn't it? Worse still, some of these side effects looked a lot like the symptoms of a heart attack: Chest pain, rapid or irregular heartbeat, tingling hands or feet, just the type of symptoms that hypochondria thrives on. I was having reservations already.

But the website did say that these symptoms were extremely rare, the main side effect being a rash in the area of application, which could be combated with certain anti-inflammatory shampoos.

Fuck it, I'll give it a go, I thought.

Ten minutes later I had bought myself an eight month supply of Minoxidil on Ebay, which rather bizarrely came with a free four month supply of Colgate toothpaste too. All for the princely sum of forty five pounds. I wasn't sure if this was a bargain or a rip off considering the fact that there was a sixty percent chance of me re-growing some of my hair and a similarly large chance of me having a cardiac arrest.

Finally I punched hair loss natural remedies into the search engine and clicked on a few of the links. Most of them listed something called Saw Palmetto and green tea as natural preventatives, there were a few other odd suggestions too, the most ridiculous, and pungent, of which seemed to be onion juice and apple cider vinegar.

...

Two hours later I left Holland and Barrett with a six month supply of Saw Palmetto, three large boxes of green tea and a couple of bottles of apple cider vinegar (I had plenty of onions at home already) and headed in the direction of my favourite boozer, The Mixing Tin, to celebrate a job well done. According to one website, apples were an excellent preventative measure against hair loss and I resolved to drink nothing but cider and green tea from now on.

Not surprisingly the bar was empty what with it being three in the afternoon on a workday. I liked the place that way, you didn't have to wait long to get served.

'Hi Marty,' I greeted the owner. 'How's business?'
'Steady, you know. How come you're not working?'
'I'm on the sick mate.'
'Oh yeah, what's wrong with you now?'
'Don't ask.'
'OK. What you drinking?'
'Pint of cider please mate.'
'Dry or sweet?'
'Don't know. Which one's got the most apple content in it?'
'Dry probably.'
'That's what I'll have then.'
He pulled the drink and placed it in front of me.
'How long you think you'll be off for?'
'Dunno, six months or so.'
'Shit mate, you have got the best job in the world.'
'It could be worse Marty, it could be worse.'

Chapter 3

I have absolutely no idea why we dream, nor have I any idea what our dreams mean, but I do know this; some weird shit goes down when I'm sleeping. One minute I'm driving my car down some country road, next thing I know I'm on a boat, in the middle of the ocean with people swimming all around it. The place looks like it might be the Caribbean or someplace like that, really light blue water, same as the sky. There's girls here too, loads of them and they're calling me into the water. Some of them aren't wearing bikinis and I can see their breasts lifting with the waves.

'Come in,' they call. 'What's wrong with you? The water's beautiful.'

I want to jump in but I'm scared. If I jump in they'll see that I'm wearing a toupee so I just watch from the side of the boat while they tease me from the impossibly blue waters. There are men in there too and eventually the women turn their attention away from me to the guys that are splashing around with them. All of a sudden everyone's getting it on in the water and the sound of dozens of people moaning floats up to the deck where I am left all alone. The sight and sound of them fucking away in the water turns me on and I decide to move to the other side of the boat, out of sight, to masturbate.

I'm sitting with my legs over the deck pulling away when my toupee drops into the water. Fuck. I jump in to fish it out, but it's sinking. I take a deep breath and dive to get it, but it's a yard out of reach, sinking slowly but slightly faster than I can swim. I need that toupee. I have to dive down for it. I'm quite deep now but just manage to grab it. Yes, got you. Now I've just got to get back to the surface. Shit, I didn't realise how deep I was. It's pretty dark down here but above I can see the bright blue of the sunlight hitting the surface. Swim for the blue light, I tell myself, but I'm almost out of air. My arms and legs are burning with exhaustion and my lungs are on fire. Swim for the blue light damn it.

I'm not going to make it.

'Jesus,' I shouted, jumping up in bed, covered in sweat, my heart pounding.

Oh, a dream. But the blue light was still there. What the fuck? Ah, the tanning lamp. I must have fallen asleep with it on. I staggered up and switched the lamp off, plunging my room into pitch darkness as I did so. Strange, it can't be that late, I thought. I got home at about half past three in the afternoon and it didn't get dark until after nine.

But my clock confirmed that it was indeed eleven thirty PM. Christ on a bike, I had been under that lamp for eight hours. Oh well, if eight hours wouldn't take the glow off the patch nothing would. Not to worry.

It proved impossible to get back to sleep so I decided to masturbate. My conscious fantasies being a lot kinder and more predictable than my sub-conscious, I was able to join in the fun and games this time. When I'd emptied myself across my stomach I got up and jumped into the shower. I didn't really want to shampoo my hair after the last holocaust that had been visited by the shower so I decided to stick to a simple rinsing instead.

'AAAGGHHRRR,' I screamed as the warm water hit my scalp. It felt as though someone were tipping hot coffee on me. 'Oh, sweet Jesus…what the hell was that?'

I soon found out. An alignment of the two remaining mirrors in my house revealed a dark red area, where the patch of white scalp has been earlier. My God that was sore, how could I have been so stupid, falling asleep under the tanning lamp?

I spent the next two hours applying and reapplying abundant amounts of moisturiser in a crude attempt to soothe the burning, but it was no good. The moisturiser seemed to turn into cooking fat the moment it touched my scalp and I eventually surmised that it may in fact be braising the top of my head. There was only one thing for it; I would have to go to accident and emergency at the hospital.

...

Due to my hypochondria I have been in hospital many, many times; usually for some scan or another. It is a sad fact of my short life that I have never once, not fucking once, had a sexy looking nurse attend to me or even a remotely good looking one for that matter. I had instead been attended to and roughly manhandled by a succession of swamp hogs, and it was a sad reflection on the state of the NHS that today was no exception.

A huge, walrus of a woman, named Janice, who just about managed to squeeze herself into her size twenty uniform, took my details and asked me what the nature of my problem was.

'I have had a nasty burn,' I informed the elephant.

'Whereabouts?'

'My scalp,' I replied, removing my cap and bowing my head to reveal the damage.

'Oh, I see. And how did the accident happen?'

I wasn't about to give this bitch a reason to mock me.

'I spilt coffee on my head.'

'Hgmmph.'

'Sorry,' I remarked. 'Was that a snigger? Is something funny?'

'No sir, not at all. Just take a seat over here and we'll get someone to see you as soon as possible.'

'Is there any chance I could get a male doctor?'

'You have something against women doctors?'

'No, it's just that I have something private I need to discuss.'

'I'll see what I can do.'

I surveyed the waiting room; it was horrible, worse than the bloody library. Many of the fucks in there were casualties of war, the bloody faces and broken arms were evidently the results of a night on the town ending in a brawl. Some moaned quietly in pain, while others complained loudly and drunkenly about how long hey had been waiting to be seen. Here and there a few of the casualties were squabbling amongst themselves and the hospital security guards were keeping a watchful eye for the first signs of any real trouble. The place would definitely kick off at some point. I just hoped it was after I had gone.

Two hours later I was finally assigned a doctor, a round faced burly eastern European man with a fat moustache who introduced himself as Dr Chalmovsky. His English was reasonable, but heavily accented.

'Please sit here Mr Hisky.'

I sat and removed my hat.

'It's burned quite badly Mr Hisky. Second degree burns, perhaps.'

'Shit, will it heal OK?'

'Over time perhaps. I'll give you some ointment that you will need to apply twice a day, every day. But there may still be a little scarring.'

'Will my hair be able to grow there again?'

'I think not, you seem to be in an advancing stage of Androgenetic Alopecia.'

My heart leapt and the sweat tap in my palms switched itself on. I knew what that meant.

'Oh dear God, no!! Can you operate?'

'No, we don't operate on Alopecia.'

'Don't operate! Oh fuck me no, please…how long have I got?'

'It's impossible to say, a few years maybe.'

I started to weep, softly at first, then loud and angry.

'I feel sick…how can this not have been spotted by my GP? I see the bastard on a monthly basis. Why the hell didn't he notice?'

'He probably didn't want to be rude.'

'Rude? Who gives a fuck about manners when a life is at stake?'

'It's hardly the end of the world Mr Hisky.'

'What?' I demanded, incredulously. 'You tell me I have inoperable skin cancer and you think that it's hardly the end of the world? Well it is for me you fucking arsehole.'

'Mr Hisky I didn't tell you that you have skin cancer. I told you that you had an advanced stage of Androgenetic Alopecia.'

'Isn't that skin cancer?'

'No it isn't.'

'Then what the fuck is it?'

'Hair loss.'

'Why the hell didn't you just say hair loss? What's with the fucking Polish? Speak English you foreign bastard.'

'I was speaking English, it is the medical term.' He was clearly upset now. Maybe I shouldn't have brought his ethnicity into it. 'But if you prefer plain English, that is fine. YOU, MR HISKY ARE GOING BALD. YOU ARE LOSING YOUR HAIR!'

'Alright, alright, tell me something I don't know. How do you think I burned myself in the first place?'

'You spilt coffee on your head.'
'…'
'…'
'Just give me my fucking ointment.'

Chapter 4

My bold experiment with the tanning lamp had failed wretchedly and now I had nothing to do about the so-called alopecia until the consignment of Minoxidil arrived. Well nothing except the thrice-daily applications of the ointment that soothed the burning that is.

After a week or so the pain was minimal and I could feel the scalp scabbing over. This additional disfigurement necessitated a state which I like to refer to as Perma-cap, that is the *constant* (except in the privacy of my own home) wearing of one of my collection of trucker hats.

To paraphrase a great saying, a week is a long time in hair loss, particularly when you are waiting for a batch of hair restoring products to arrive. I felt that by sitting doing nothing I was losing ground, every second might count for all I knew. There were one hundred and seventeen hairs in the bathtub that morning, the fucking thing looked like a barber's floor and I felt that at this rate I would be looking like Telly Savalis by the time those Indian ebay-ers got my Minoxidil to me. It might therefore be a good idea to look at some drastic options, like hair transplants, just in case.

Another trip to the library would be required.

...

The library reeked as bad as ever, but was not quite so full for a change, in fact the terminals to the left and right of me were unoccupied, which made me feel less self-conscious about typing hair loss into the search engine. The first thing that popped up was a sponsored link to a place called the Hair Loss Centre. I surfed my way past the shit about Minoxodil and Propecia and headed straight for surgical hair replacement.

There seemed to be two options available, hair replacement, which I liked the sound of and scalp reduction which, from what I could make out, seemed to involve ripping out the bald part of your scalp and sewing the loose ends around it together. The website went on to explain that tearing off my scalp in this way 'may be painful.' There was no *may* about it; that shit *had* to hurt. It also said that this surgery could lead to scarring or infection, but more importantly that it was expensive and once again not available on the NHS. What was it with the fucking NHS? Why did they discriminate against bald people in this way? Why was it that it was possible to get a breast enlargement, or turn yourself from a perfectly normal man into a woman with an Adam's Apple and a pair of bollocks, yet you couldn't get yourself a hair transplant? As far as I was concerned baldness should pretty much be considered a disability.

Equal rights for slap heads man.

A quick scan through a few other websites revealed that most clinics didn't even bother to give you a price. You had to send in an enquiry. I knew what that meant, some expert salesman would ring back telling me how a hair transplant would transform my life, how it 'only cost' ten grand and how shitty my life would be if I carried on without getting myself treated. I didn't need that sort of twat depressing me so I persevered until I found one site bold enough to publish their prices. Unfortunately it was a New York based centre, but at least it might give me an idea about how much it might cost. The site displayed a chart, called the Norwood Scale, which depicted a series of heads in various stages of hairlessness, each of which had a code. I entered the code which I felt matched my own condition and waited for the price to come back. Eight thousand US dollars. Not too bad considering the current exchange rate, but still more than I had to spend.

Perhaps a second job might be in order. It wouldn't be so bad; after all I still had five and a half months of sick leave ahead of me. I could quite easily get a second full time job for the next few months. Preferably one that allowed me to wear a cap. Might as well search the employment sections in the newspapers while I'm here, I thought.

I did the math. At the current exchange rate eight thousand dollars came to approximately five thousand pounds. That was a grand a month that I needed to save, which was more than feasible, my wage from the council would be for living on and any second income could be banked for a transplant.

Simple.

The jobs section was mostly full of career type jobs or call centre work, neither of which appealed to me. A call centre had to be the most soulless place in the world to work and any job that advertised itself as a career would no doubt have a lengthy recruitment process. I needed an immediate start. Aha, what was this under the Hotel and Catering section? Night Porter in busy city centre urgently required. Urgently meant immediate, so I punched the number into my mobile phone, finished scanning the jobs pages for other options, of which there were none, and dumped the papers back in the rack. I then left the library and used my mobile to call the Premier Travel Inn.

'Good afternoon, Premier Travel Inn, Leeds. This is Janet speaking, how can I help?'

'Oh, good afternoon I'm phoning about the Night Porter's job you have advertised in the Evening Post.'

'Can I just take your name please?'

'Yes, it's Paul Hisky.'

'Hold the line a minute Paul.'

'OK.'

I listened to some shitty piped music for about twenty seconds or so and then a second voice answered the phone.

'Hello Paul, This is Brent Hutchins, the General Manager speaking.'

'Hi, I was just telling the lady. I'm phoning about the Night Porter's job you have advertised in the Evening Post.'

'Yes, do you have any experience?'

'I have several years experience of working in the catering industry, but no actual Night Porter experience. How hard can it be?'

'You'd be surprised Paul. It carries quite a lot of responsibility. You are the person in charge of the whole hotel between the hours of ten at night and six in the morning. If there are any problems you have to deal with them.'

'That wouldn't be a problem, I am a very responsible person,' I lied. 'I have worked in supervisory positions at various times in my career.'

'And you're not working now?'

'Actually I am studying for a master's degree. I have taken a year out of the rat race to complete it. I thought a night job would be ideal.'

Another lie.

'When could you come down for an interview?' Brent asked.

'Well, I'm in town now, but I have just finished at university and I'm not in a suit or anything, just my regular clothes.'

'Well if you come down this afternoon I can interview you then.'

'Yes I can be there in about half an hour,' I replied.

'Excellent, see you soon.'

'Yes see you, thanks, and bye.'

This Brent character sounded anxious to get someone signed up. Urgently required the advert had said. That reeked of desperation. This job was mine.

I went straight back into the library and grabbed the meatiest looking textbook I could find, one about the French Revolution, signed it out and stuck it under my arm; then waltzed off to the Premier Travel Inn to dupe Brent into giving me a job.

...

The interview only lasted about ten minutes. Brent, who wore thick glasses and had an un-naturally round face, kept yawning the whole way through. No doubt the moonfaced bastard was having to cover some of the shifts himself. Little wonder they *urgently* needed someone. It wasn't much of an interview really; Brent just told me what the job involved and then asked me if I had any questions.

'Will I be allowed to read my textbooks at the desk, when there are no guests around?' I asked.

'That wouldn't be a problem, as long the fire checks are completed every half hour.'

I didn't have any more questions, except, 'When can I start?'

'Well I do have a couple of other people to interview,' he replied.

I didn't believe him, but I guess he couldn't give me the job there and then.

'But I will let you know by tomorrow.'

'Thanks Brent,' I said, standing up and shaking his hand enthusiastically. He returned it, limply. The poor bastard was shattered.

Chapter 5

I found out the next day that the job was indeed mine. Brent covered his bases by telling me I would be on a six-week trial period and that my training would commence that very weekend. Ten PM sharp. No problem I had told him, I was looking forward to it.

Couldn't wait.

Then two days after Brent's call the Minoxidil arrived. It did so in a large bubble wrapped envelope, covered (and I mean covered) in Indian postage stamps. Christ, it was a wonder they had managed to find a space in which to write my address. Did those guys not have stamps in denominations higher than five rupees?

I unwrapped the miracle grow eagerly and settled down to the instructions, re-reading the list of possible side effects first before moving on to the obvious warnings. Avoid drinking …blah blah… contact with eyes, etc etc. What fucker puts hair growing solution in their mouth or eyes?

The Minoxidil came with a dropper that had to be filled to one millilitre and then applied evenly to the area of the scalp that was balding. This had to be done twice a day and purportedly four out of five men experienced re-growth within four months using this method. Please God don't let me be one of the twenty percent that didn't.

Most of the scabs from my burns had started peeling off and I decided to go for it and apply the lotion straight away, but first I had to wash out the onion juice I had been using for the last two days, mainly because I was afraid it might neutralise the Minoxidil but also because it fucking stank to high heaven.

One application of Minoxidil Extra Strength and four strong cups of green tea later, I decided to get up and treat myself to a few ciders down at my favourite bar, The Mixing Tin, to celebrate the first step on my road to recovery. A tsunami of optimism flooded through me and for the first time since I had been diagnosed as terminally hairless I saw the faintest light at the end of my dark, lonely tunnel. I might just have a reason to live after all.

As always during the day, the bar was empty. Except that is for the bartender, Marty. He was busying himself practicing his bottle spinning routine behind the bar. He was pretty good at that Tom Cruise, *Cocktail* shit but to be honest I found it all a bit Eighties. I was clearly in the minority though, as the ten thousand legions of Marty's harem would no doubt testify. The bastard was laying a different girl on a nightly basis due to his feats of skill with a Havana Club bottle and a silver tin. Though it might also have something to do with him giving the best looking girls free drinks.

'Hi Marty, pint of cider please mate.'

'Alright mate,' he replied. 'You never guess who was in here earlier.'

'Who?' I enquired.

'Doctor Rossi.'

'Fuck off.'

'He was and he asked about you too. Apparently he's back home for his grandmother's funeral.'

Doctor Rossi, my old drinking buddy. He wasn't actually a doctor at all; he dropped out of medical school after the second year. Not because he wasn't bright enough, not even because he couldn't afford to carry on studying. Doctor Rossi dropped out because, like me, worse than me actually, he suffered from severe hypochondria. Can you imagine how bad it must be learning about all these weird and wonderful illnesses everyday if you have severe hypochondria? The poor bastard thought he had everything, the last time I saw him he had been convinced he was suffering from something called Ebola, a flesh eating disease found in Africa. He had been hysterical for about three days, quarantining himself in his room until Taylor, one of our mutual friends, pointed out that it wasn't a flesh eating disease at all; it was a cigarette burn that he had sustained while drinking about sixteen pints of beer and passing out on Taylor's couch with a cigarette in his mouth.

Doctor Rossi.

The good doctor, real name Mark Rossi had shot through to Manchester shortly afterwards to study chemistry instead. He planned to finish his degree and then undertake a PHD, thereby finally achieving his lifelong ambition of having the title Dr before his name. I had deliberately avoided contact with him since he left. Hypochondriacs should never mix in a social capacity. You feed off each other's neurosis. I had never even heard of a panic attack until that bastard started telling me about his, and then all of a sudden I start having them. Panic attacks are quite possibly the only illness you can actually manifest yourself, they feed on hypochondria and I had Rossi to blame for two years of being monged out of my brain on tranquillisers. I had no intention of getting mixed up with him again.

'Where is he staying?' I asked.
'At his mother's house apparently.'
'Shit.'
'What's wrong with that?'
'His mother lives two doors down from my mother.'
'So?'
'So he'll ask my mother my new address.'
'Is that bad?'
'Real bad Marty, real bad.'

...

I stayed in the bar until five thirty, when it started to fill up with suits finishing work. The clientele were mostly lawyers and professional types, nothing like me at all. I didn't really want to go home just yet but by the same token I didn't want to spend too much money while I had an urgent operation to save for.

I picked up a four-pack of cider and a copy of Men's Health and a newspaper from the supermarket and headed home. Once home I cracked open a can of the cider and opened the newspaper heading straight for the sport section. Liverpool were playing in Europe that night and I made a note to watch it at seven forty five. After I finished reading the sports pages I picked up my copy of Men's Health and began to browse through the pages.

After the 'Keeping Her Satisfied' feature, the article that caught my attention next was the magazine's Short Story Competition. Not that I had any literary aspirations of which to speak, but with a ten thousand pound first prize at stake I was willing to give it a shot. The theme was 'Embarrassing Visits to Your Doctor' of which, quite frankly, I'd had my fair share. So I dusted down the old word processor that I had stored under my bed and began to rank my medical history from slightly humiliating to utterly mortifying. The tests on my prostate had been particularly undignified, as had the twisted testicle, but try as I might I just could get started on a two thousand word story on either of these subjects. Instead my mind kept drifting to the burnt scalp incident I had recently been through. Of course, a burnt scalp wouldn't be particularly embarrassing unless I set the scene with the discovery that I was losing my hair.

Two hours later I had regaled the whole hair loss horror story onto the blank white sheets that I'd stuffed into the word processor and slipped the finished story into an envelope, ready to post the next day. Ten grand, I mused, dreaming of the flowing tresses that I could afford to have implanted into my scalp with that amount of money. I was so excited by the prospect that I could scarcely concentrate on the other articles in my magazine. In fact I skipped straight past 'Boosting Your IQ', 'Blasting Your Fat' and 'Keeping Her Satisfied' and turned instead to the advertising section in the back, a section that consisted almost entirely of penis enlargement, impotence, dating and baldness advertisements. Was that where we were grouped? I noted with dismay. We slapheads, right next to the needle dicks, lonely hearts and the blokes that couldn't get it up? What a fucking depressing state of affairs. Still, you had to hand it to the advertisers, they knew what they were doing, place anyone alongside this bunch of misfits and they'll buy whatever it is you're selling just to disassociate themselves from the other type of so called 'losers'. No doubt some poor fucker with a dick like a pre-pubescent Stuart Little was currently staring at this section of the magazine, incredulous at the fact that the advertisers had grouped him with the bald brigade.

Chapter 6

What a game, Liverpool had been three nil down at half time, before somehow making a miraculous comeback to draw three all at full time. Extra time and penalties loomed. Absolutely remarkable. Unfortunately, here was the most exciting game I had ever watched in my life and my cider cans were all now lying empty on the floor beside my couch. I would have to run down to the corner shop while the players were waiting for extra time.

I picked up my coat and cap and darted, full speed, down to the local grocery store. The place was still open, thank God, and it looked like a number of other people had the same idea as me. There were several customers in there with arms full of beer waiting to be served.

I pushed through the queue and made my way to the cider section, picking up a two-litre bottle of Strongbow before taking my place at the back of the queue.

'My dear sweet brother Hisky,' came a familiar greeting from behind me in the shop.

'Doctor Rossi I presume,' I replied keeping my back to him so that he wouldn't see the grimace on my face or me mouthing the word *shit*.

'Watching the game are you?'

'Er, yeah.' I replied turning to face him.

'You look well,' he remarked.

'You too,' I lied. He had gone grey, real grey, since I had last seen him. He looked like he had put on a bit of weight too.

'Where are you watching it? At home?' he enquired.

'Yeah.'

'Alone?'

'Yeah.'

'I'll come round and keep you company.'

Just fucking great.
'Nice one. You got any booze?'
'Nah, just some snacks. I've stopped drinking.'
'Why?'
'Liver problems.'
So that's what he's got this week, I thought.
'Really?'
'Yeah.'
'So do you have to go to hospital?'
'Nah, the hospital have done scans but claim they can't find anything wrong. Useless twats.'
It's funny but sometimes, when I spoke to Doctor Rossi I could quite easily see the ridiculousness of his hypochondria. Yet somehow I couldn't stop myself from acting in a similarly neurotic manner.
'You should stop drinking too.'
'I don't want to.'
'Do you know what that shit does to your liver, not to mention your kidneys.'
'Look I don't want to know OK. I have no intention of quitting drinking. You already got me to stop smoking, against my will I might add. Leave me one fucking pleasure in life will you.'
'OK, OK, calm down.'
'I am calm, now hurry up and grab your snacks and get a move on. I don't want to miss any of this game.'

…

Rossi can be an irritating bastard. Not only does he an annoying habit of informing you about the perils of weird and wonderful diseases but he also talks constantly, about shit. He never knows when to shut up. Here I was trying to watch Andriy Shevchenko lining up a spot kick against the

Liverpool keeper, which if missed would hand Liverpool the most famous victory the cup had ever seen and here was this bastard trying to talk to me about the war in Iraq!

'Rossi! Shut up for two minutes. I thought you came here to watch the bloody game.'

He didn't like being called Rossi, it had to be Mark or Doctor Rossi.

'OK, I'm just off to the toilet anyway.'

'Yeah, OK,' I muttered as I concentrated on the penalty. Shevchenko ran up and hit the ball.

'Miss you fucker…Yeeeessss,' I screamed as Dudek saved the ball on the line. I jumped up screaming and shouting, dancing across the living room. Here was surely one of the greatest sporting spectacles of all time. The toilet flushed and Rossi re-appeared from the door. I would have given him a hug but he'd not even washed his hands, the dirty fucker, so I simply shouted 'YEESSSS' again at him.

'They won it?' he asked.

'They fucking well did.'

'That's amazing.'

'You're not wrong Rossi this is unbelievable.'

'So how long have you been going bald for?'

What the fuck? That brought me down with a bang.

'Eh? What are you talking about?'

'I just spotted the bottle of Minoxidil on your bathroom shelf.'

Shit, fuck! I'd have to remember to hide that in future.

'So are you going to tell me how long you've been going bald for?' he repeated. I'm sure I noticed a slight smirk on his face, probably getting revenge for me calling him Rossi instead of Mark or Doctor.

'I don't know,' I said sitting down again. 'I only realised a couple of weeks ago.' From the corner of my eye I could

see Steven Gerrard and the rest of the Liverpool players joyously hugging each other on the pitch in Istanbul.
'Personally, I didn't feel like celebrating anymore.
'So how long have you been on the Minoxidil?'
'Only two days.'
'You won't have noticed any side effects yet then?'
'No, except my scalp itches a bit after I apply the stuff.'
'Yeah, I know that's one of the major side effects, along with a racing heart beat and…'
'Enough! I know all about the side effects. I don't want to talk about those anymore.'
'Well you know you can get some shampoos that combat the itchy scalp don't you?'
'I didn't actually. Anyway, how come you know so much about Minoxidil?'
'I'm studying chemistry aren't I?'
'I thought that was all about magnesium and PH values and shit.'
'It is about that shit but that's the type of shit that gets used to make formulas such as Minoxidil. In fact I have actually thought about making my own Minoxidil as well as other topical solutions for baldness.'
'Why, you're not bald?'
'Yes but millions of men in this country alone are. That's where the money is mate, preying on human misery.'
'Great, so do you reckon this Minoxidil will actually work?'
'To an extent. It's best to use it in conjunction with Propecia and Nizoral to optimise re-growth but of course that also optimises the risk of side effects.'
'What's Nizoral?'
'That's a shampoo that contains something called Ketoconazole, which is a type of anti-androgen.'

'Woah, woah, you're losing me now. Don't give me all this chemistry jargon.'
'Basically it stops your hair from falling out.'
'What? Why didn't my doctor tell me this?'
'Well it's not been tested as a hair loss product, it is simply marketed as an anti dandruff shampoo. It is also an excellent anti-inflammatory, which means it will relieve the itching you get from your Minoxidil. So at worst it will help the itching and at best it might stop your condition from worsening. Not only that but if only used twice a week there are no adverse effects whatsoever.'
'Fuck me, you mean this could all have been prevented?'
'Not necessarily. It depends on your susceptibility to male pattern baldness. Some people are destined to look like Zinedine Zidane, while others might just be able to slow the enemy down as long as they are willing to put the time, effort and money into a hair maintenance regime.'
'I'm willing.'
'Good, then you might just have a shot at keeping your mane. I recommend you get on the Propecia too, for optimum re-growth.'
'I'm not so sure about the tablets mate. Remember what happened when I took those malaria tablets.'
'How could I forget?'
The malaria tablets had been a particularly colourful episode in my history of hypochondria. The list of possible side effects had been horrendous:

- *blurred vision, or change in vision (sometimes reversible)*
- *fainting spells*
- *fever or chills*
- *hearing problems*
- *headaches, confusion, or other mental changes*
- *joint or muscle aches*

•redness, blistering, peeling or loosening of the skin, including inside the mouth
•ringing in the ears
•seizures (convulsions)
•skin rash, itching (there may be severe itching without a rash)
•unusual changes in heart rate or other heart problems
•unusual tiredness or weakness
•vomiting

Seizures! Change in vision (sometimes reversible)! So other times not then! Heart problems! Is it any wonder I ended up in Accident and Emergency, with electrodes strapped all over my body. They thought I was having a heart attack, I certainly thought I was, as I repeatedly chanted the Lord's Prayer in terror. It turned out it was just a really serious panic attack, which are also associated with anti-malarial drugs. So I wasn't overly keen to go down the tablets route again, not if there were side effects anyway.

'Aren't there any treatments without side effects?'

'Well I'm not sure myself what the side effects from Propecia are, I'll have to find out. There are other topical options, but they are expensive. Of course we could try making some ourselves, that would cut costs dramatically.'

'You mean you want me to be your guinea pig?'

'Nah mate, more of a lab rat than a guinea pig.'

'Real funny.'

'Don't worry pal, we'll have you looking like Ozzy Osbourne in no time.'

I hoped to God he meant the hair and not the drug induced pallor, limp arms and slurred speech.

Chapter 7

Rossi attended his grandmother's funeral the next day before leaving for Manchester again. He gave me his new phone number and told me to expect an email from him the following week, after he had researched a few other topical therapies for me.

In the meantime I had a new job to start and I set about the task of seeing which hairstyle would best cover the scabby, bald, patch of skin at the back of my head. I could plonk a cap on my head the minute the rest of the staff were out of the hotel, but would have to actually turn up to work without one.

My hair was about three inches long and pretty limp to say the least. I had always styled it in a centre parting but the narrow river of white scalp running from the front of my head to the back, now looked like it had burst its banks and culminated in a huge scab encrusted lake at my vertex. The centre parting had to go.

The obvious choice was an LSP (or lower side parting), which would act as a type of comb-over, covering the bald spot. I was acutely aware of the ridiculousness of these comb-over hairstyles on severely bald men, but surely it wouldn't look so bad if you were merely aiming to cover a bald spot rather than the full head. I decided to give it a go.

I looked ridiculous. By some cruel twist of fate the bald spot appeared to be worse at the left side of my vertex, which made the traditional left to right parting impossible. I had to part it from right to left, which left me looking somewhat like Hitler without his moustache.

My next idea was to wax the hair and slick it straight back, greasy Italian style, and hope that the long hairs from the front covered the bald area at the back. They didn't. Shit. Worse still, the task of washing out the greasy wax precipitated an almighty shed, which only served to dishearten me further.

I toyed with the idea of just shaving the whole lot off, but given my scrawny frame choosing skin as a hairstyle seemed even less attractive than looking like the Fuhrer minus the moustache. It would have to be the LSP.

The next step was to pay a visit to my local pharmacy and get some of this Nizoral shit that Rossi had been talking about. My scalp was itching like a prostitutes privates and huge chunks of white dandruff had been flaking off my head. I wasn't sure whether it was the Minoxidil or the scabs from my altercation with the tanning lamp, but either way an anti-inflammatory would have to be added to the regimen.

The Nizoral cost me £7.99 which wasn't too bad considering it was supposed to last for three months and that Rossi reckoned it had re-growth properties as well. I also purchased some L'Oreal Thickening Conditioner and while browsing the rest of the store noticed some self-tanning moisturiser on sale. Of course, why hadn't I thought of that before? I could ditch the cancer lamp and use this self-tanning shit instead.

Genius.

Back at the flat I took another shower and made my first application of the Nizoral, which I have to say did an excellent job of easing the irritation to my scalp. I then applied a healthy dose of the self-tanning lotion to my patch and face, figuring I might as well give the old phizog a healthy glow as well.

Night came and at nine-thirty I readied myself for work. A uniform would be provided but in the meantime I was supposed to wear a white shirt and black trousers. I combed my hair into the Hitler parting, gave myself a little Nazi salute in the mirror and stuck a cap in my rucksack, ready to plonk on my head as soon as the rest of the staff had left.

...

Brent wasn't there when I arrived; he had apparently been on a day shift and left a message that he would see me the following morning at six. In the meantime I would be given an induction by Samantha, a receptionist. Samantha informed me that she would be working with me for the entire duration of my shift and that starting tomorrow I would be on my own.

'Oh. I thought I would be alone tonight too,' I informed her.

'Not tonight love,' she replied, glancing at my LSP disapprovingly. 'You'll need someone to show you round the whole hotel. It's very important that the fire checks are done properly, every half hour and that you know where to check.'

'Fine,' I replied, cursing the fact that I would have to remain cap less for the duration of the night. Worse still, this Samantha character was quite fit. She had dark Mediterranean face, long dark hair, slender and an enormous bosom. Why the fuck had I gone with the side parting? Because I had expected Brent or that ugly Janet character to be working, not Catherine Zeta Jones.

'OK,' the sexy bitch announced. 'Let's give you the tour of the hotel shall we.'

'Er, do you mind if I use the bathroom first?'

'No, not at all. It's just through there.' She pointed through a door at the side of reception, which led to the hotel's rooms and the staff bathroom.

I entered the bathroom then pulled out my hair brush and quickly set to work rearranging the LSP into a centre parting once more. I couldn't check on my hair/scalp ratio without a vanity mirror and cursed myself for not buying one from the pharmacy.

'OK I'm ready,' I said as I strode back into the reception.

'Let's go then,' Samantha replied, staring at my hastily re-organised mane. 'It's just through this door.'

'After you,' I insisted, eager to keep her in front of me where she wouldn't spot the patch.

'Age before beauty,' she answered.

'No, really. You first.' I wasn't going to back down.

'OK, follow me.'

I spent the rest of the tour hovering about a meter behind Sam's left shoulder as she led me through the hotel explaining exactly what my duties would entail. She seemed a little disconcerted at the fact that wherever she moved I aligned my body so that I was facing her, smiling innocently as I did so.

Eventually we returned to the reception desk where we sat side by side in two swivel chairs. I swivelled my chair to an angle where I thought she wouldn't see my vertex and we began to chat.

'So how long have you worked here?' I asked.

'Three years, I'm leaving in December to do a round the world trip.'

'Really, I just came back from one about a month ago.' It wasn't a complete lie, I had actually made a round the world trip four years ago.

'I thought you looked a bit tanned,' Sam noted.

'Do I? Huh, I thought it had worn off by now. Where's your first port of call?'

'Hong Kong.'

'Nice. You'll love it there,' I said, nodding sagely. 'I guess it's over to Bangkok after that?'

'Yeah, how did you guess?'

'It's the classic route.'

I had a captive audience now, as I regaled her with tales of the Orient, many of which were tales I had heard from other backpackers but I skilfully managed to insert myself as the protagonist.

'Wow, I can't wait,' the awe struck vixen sighed as I finished a particularly amusing tale involving myself, a Chinese restaurateur and a stolen bicycle.

'So are you going with your boyfriend?'

'No, I don't have one.'

Bingo.

'Huh, no boyfriend. You a bit of a free spirit are you?'

'You could say that…'

We spent the next two hours talking about travel and places that we both wanted to visit before moving on to the subject of relationships. Sam hadn't had a proper boyfriend for two years, basically ever since she had split up with her childhood sweetheart, who she had been with for six years. I informed her that the longest I had ever been with a girl was for eight months, which she wouldn't believe. I was definitely in here, I mused.

By three in the morning I was fading fast and so was Samantha. We yawned and smiled at each other.

'Ooh, time for the fire check,' I announced.

'You're learning,' she replied. 'I'll do this one myself though, I need the toilet anyway. You watch the desk and then you can do the next check yourself in half an hour.'

'OK love, no problem. Shout me if you need me.'

'I think I should be OK Paul. I have been here for three years remember.'

I watched her wiggle her magnificent posterior through the door and sighed when she was out of earshot.

'I would fucking love to,' I told myself.

…

'Paul. Wake up love. Paul.'

'Huh?'

'You've fallen asleep while I was doing the fire check,' she explained laughing.

My God I had. I'd dropped off with my face on the desk, displaying the scabby scalp of shame to all and sundry. Sam stood above me sniggering.

'What? What's so funny?'

It must be the patch.

'Nothing. Just you, falling asleep on your first day,' she replied, belly laughing now.

'It's not that funny.'

'It is.' The bitch was in hysterics

'Why do you find that so funny?' I demanded folding my arms and moving my chair back to the wall to shield my shame.

'You just looked funny that's all.'

'Funny how?'

'Just funny.'

What did you see? I wanted to scream like a demented Gestapo agent, how much do you know? Talk bitch, talk!

'Well I'm glad you find it so amusing,' I sulked.

'What's wrong? You just looked funny.'

'Yeah, I bet I did. Lap it up. Go on keep laughing.'

'Jesus, what the hell's wrong with you?'

'You know what.'

'Do I?'

'…'

'Fine, be like that. We've only got another two and a half hours before I finish anyway. Thank God I'm not working with you tomorrow, you moody bastard.'

Chapter 8

All things considered, the first night hadn't gone well at all. I'd managed to piss off my very attractive colleague *and* flaunt my bald spot to her at the same time. On top of that; Brent was running late the next morning and had the audacity to phone ahead and request that I wait around for him until he arrived. Apparently he wanted to grill me on how my first night went.

'Fine,' I told him when he eventually arrived, almost an hour late. 'By the way am I getting paid for still being here?'

No, was the short answer to that one. He spouted some shit about me being a trainee and in a probationary period and that it was imperative that I be monitored for my progress etc. Progress? Wasn't this a job as a night porter? What progress was I expected to make exactly?

When he eventually did let me go it was almost eight o' clock in the morning and the adrenalin of the anger I felt at being forced to wait for cock-face Brent meant I no longer felt tired. Instead I popped into town for a cooked breakfast of sausage, egg, bacon and beans and then waited outside the library for it to open its doors. Which it did two minutes late at nine o' two.

'About fucking time,' I muttered under my breath at the freaky looking attendant that opened the doors.

I followed him as he lurched towards his counter and noted how similar he looked to Emmett Brown from *Back to the Future* with his eccentric shock of grey hair.

'Internet?' the Emmett Brown look-alike asked.

'No I've actually come here to borrow your flux capacitor.'

'Oh, I don't know if we have a copy of that. One moment I'll just check the system. Do you know the author?'

'…Er…Try Marty Mc Fly.'
'Is that Mac or Mc?'
'Mc I think.'
'No, we don't seem to have a copy of that one. Sorry.'
'Not to worry, I'll just book an hour on the internet instead please.'

…

My inbox was full of the usual shit. Enhance Your Performance, Enlarge Your Penis, Give It To Her All Night etc. There was however one proper email from the good Doctor Rossi that was titled *Hair Loss Solutions*. I clicked on the email and began to read.

Hi Mate, how you doing?

I've been doing a bit of research into the type of products on the market that might be suitable for you. I know you don't want me to bore you with technical details so I'll briefly outline (in layman's terms) what the root causes of male pattern baldness are. I'll then give you a list of the products that I would be taking if I were unfortunate enough to be disfigured by hair loss myself.

Basically the cause of your hair loss is your testicles. They produce a specialised form of testosterone. Dihydrotestosterone (or DHT) affects hair as it grows, resulting in the production of fewer and shorter hairs. The hair follicles begin to decrease in diameter (a process known as miniaturisation). Results vary, but hair grown from smaller hair follicles tends to be lighter in colour, and eventually the narrowing follicles stop producing hair altogether.

You've heard the myth that bald men are more virile? Well this stems from Roman times when eunuchs were kept as slaves. Eunuchs, as I am sure you are aware, were basically slaves with their balls chopped off. These poor fuckers may not have had any veg to go with their meat but by way of compensation they were saved the mental anguish of being bereaved of their hair. The same goes for the choirboys that were ritually castrated by the Catholic Church. These poor bastards were known as the Castrati and were deprived of their codlings in order to keep their voices high pitched. Oh and before you go signing up for choir practice I must point out that this whole barbaric procedure was abolished in 1878 by Pope Leo.

I know what you are thinking: Will a vasectomy stop my hair falling out? Well the answer to that my bald friend is no. You would have to actually hack your nuts off in order to achieve that aim and I doubt even you would go to that length.

Therefore it seems to me that your best course of action would be to get on a drug that reduces DHT as soon as possible. Unfortunately the only FDA approved drug that does this is Propecia, which you have already told me you are reluctant to take. But when you look at the side effects they are not exactly life threatening. True this stuff can have a serious effect on the libido and cause impotence in a small number of users, but as it is painfully evident that you will not be using your dick very often as a slap head you might as well give it a go anyway.

It seems that the combination of Nizoral, (which I recommended to you earlier) and the Minoxidil, that you are already on, along with Propecia is the single most effective (proven) treatment going. There are a number of topical treatments that purportedly combat the miniaturising effects of DHT but these have not been approved by the FDA (Food and Drug Administration) which has approved the aforementioned products.

Lucky for you Propecia can be bought relatively cheaply online and if you buy something called Proscar it is even cheaper still. Proscar is actually the exact same drug but in 5mg form as opposed to the 1mg form of Propecia. All you have to do is cut each tablet up into fifths and hey presto you have yourself a cheap batch of hair restorer.

Hope this helps,

Doctor Rossi

Doh, almost forgot here are the unproven topicals:

Revivogen
Crinagen
Spironolactone

…

I minimised the email and opened up a new window. I then searched for Revivogen and found the product's homepage and clicked on order. There were several products to choose from, all of which were expensive. Three month's supply of the Anti-DHT Scalp Therapy came in at $99 while a six month supply would be $165 plus postage and packing. There were also a number of shampoos and conditioners that didn't appear to actually do anything that a regular shampoo wouldn't except cash in on the Revivogen name.

Spironolactone, my second topical option, yielded no specific product page. Just a load of medical websites informing me it was a drug used to treat women with facial hair. I certainly didn't want to be taking something that prevented hair growth, even if it was facial, so I quickly skipped to Crinagen.

Once again the product didn't seem to have its own website, instead I followed a series of links that led me to a website called Hairlosstalk.com.

At $52 for a three months supply Crinagen appeared to be the cheapest option available, though the website did have its bases covered by pointing out that while this product wasn't *actually* proven, the *science* behind it *was*. Yeah well the science behind the fucking Challenger Space Shuttle was proven too, I thought, but that didn't stop the bloody thing from bursting into a million pieces did it?

Still, I couldn't afford not to give it a try. It came under the category of DHT inhibitors and claimed that in conjunction with a growth stimulant like Minoxidil it may be successful in hair re-growth. I purchased a three month supply and began to browse the rest of the hair loss site.

The first thing to catch my eye was the link to concealing products, which took me through to two different products, Toppik and COUVRé. I clicked on COUVRé first:

With this undetectable lotion-compound nobody will ever see that your scalp is showing through, or even notice that your hair is thinning. Whether you are thinning in the front, at the crown, or anywhere else, COUVRé will eliminate the problem - instantly.

Next I clicked on Toppik:

Folks, this is our best selling product, hands down. Highly acclaimed by our members for many years, and used by people in Hollywood (no, really)... You can also drop the worries about the embarrassing 'Spray on Hair' commercials we've all seen. You'll be surprised how scientifically advanced it really is...

At twenty dollars for each of the products these seemed like an excellent short term cosmetic option. Hopefully I could conceal my bald spot until the Minoxidil and Crinagen began restoring my degenerated hairline. Delighted at this possible alternative to perma-cap I added them to the basket and proceeded to checkout. Just under a hundred USD spent, which equated to about sixty quid. In a few short weeks I'd be able to ditch the caps and get on with living my life.

Hoorah for concealers.

Chapter 9

The next five days went slowly, real slowly. In fact, if it wasn't for the cider, which I sneaked into the hotel in my rucksack, I would have quit the night porter job after the second shift. Staying awake was a real problem and I found that the only way I could do so was to masturbate once or twice during key points in the night. By the fifth shift I had pretty much worked out my routine. Start at ten; wait until all the other staff had left then crack open the first tin of Strongbow. Second can about one in the morning, first wank would be at about three, by which time most of the guests were tucked up in bed, followed by a third can of cider. The newspaper guy delivered the papers at four o' clock, which gave me an hour to read the sports sections before abusing myself for a second time.

I had been warned by Brent and Samantha that, while most of the hotel guests were business men and women, the hotel was overrun by hen and stag groups on weekends. So when my first Friday night came I made sure I had more cider in my rucksack than normal. I knew from long experience that the only way I could tolerate drunken people was to be at least semi-drunk myself. I reasoned that my best course of action would be to drink my way through the period while the pissheads were returning to the hotel, then when it died off I could sober myself up, before the day shift took over.

My body clock was getting used to the new routine by now and when I saw the amount of quality pussy coming and going from the hotel I immediately thought that this job might not be so bad after all. I took over the desk from the evening receptionist, a non-descript plump girl called Diane, who informed me that the hotel was fully booked that night.

'OK Diane, cheers,' I thanked her as I watched her waddle her fat arse towards the exit. I stared as she climbed into her car and observed the puff of smoke from the exhaust when she fired it up, before pulling away.

Cider time.

...

What a difference a day makes. At this time yesterday I had been watching grey haired suits carrying their brief cases to their rooms after staying behind at the office. Now I was watching a veritable procession of sluts heading back in after a skin-full of tart fuel. Unfortunately, there were a large number of all male stag parties too. Most of them were friendly enough but shortly after two in the morning I was disturbed by a group of seven blokes wearing Liverpool shirts ringing the bell on reception.

'YOUU REDSS!' I heard them singing as I peeked through the spy hole on my office door. Two of them were bleeding and another had what looked like it would be a considerably large black eye. They were big fuckers too, real meatheads and I wondered if there was some sort of arm-wrestling competition in town.

I toyed with the idea of just ignoring them, but they rang the bell again, several times.

'Morning lads,' I hailed them, fake smile in place as I reluctantly opened the door. 'Had a good night?'

'Fucking brilliant,' one of the grippers replied. 'Shame the clubs all shut at two though. We just wanted to know where we can get another drink from at this time mate.'

'I don't know anywhere that's open after two o clock lads.'

'You do, you lying bastard!' the one with the bruised eye shouted.

No wonder he'd been lamped, I thought, he was definitely in town for a rumble.

'I'm not lying mate, I don't know.'

'Fucking, lying, Yorkshire twat.'

'Leave him alone Rob lad,' his mate replied in his thick, Scouse accent. 'He's not done fuck all. Just calm down will you.'

I was glad there was a desk between myself and this Rob character, who was blatantly itching for another fight. Even so I did begin to plan my escape route into the back office, which I might have to use as some sort of a panic room if things did kick off.

'Yeah, shut the fuck up Rob,' added one of the lads with the nosebleed. 'I'm fucking sick of you tonight.'

I reasoned that Rob had probably started the brawl that had ended with three of them taking a beating.

'So there's nowhere open at all?' Nosebleed turned and asked me.

'Not that I know of,' I replied staring over his shoulder, at another stag party that I could see staggering towards the hotel outside.

Shit, these fuckers looked unruly as well and appeared to be chanting football songs. With this Rob character spoiling for a brawl, this was the last thing I needed, a second drunken group of football hooligans. This place was going to need a bouncer not a night porter, I thought as I edged my way towards the back office.

The second group barged through the doors, laughing and singing at the top of their voices. Rob, Nosebleed and their mates turned around to see who was making all the racket. This was my chance, get in the back, bolt the door and call the police.

'Now it's glory around the fields of Anfield Road!!!' Rob sang joyously, obviously recognising the song they were singing and joining in with it himself. 'Whehay, Champions of fucking Europe.'

Before long, from the safety of the back office I could hear them all singing along happily together. I placed the phone back on the receiver and pressed my ear against the door to listen to what they were saying.

'Here y'are lads, do you know where we can get a fucking beer at this time? Everywhere seems to shut at two.'

'Get yourselves to the knocking shop over the road!'

Of course Winston's, the brothel across the road, I thought as I eavesdropped, they no doubt had a bar.

'You mean there's a fucking meat market over the road and that fucking receptionist didn't tell us?' black-eyed Rob scowled.

I picked the phone off the cradle again, just in case.

'Useless twat, where's he gone anyway?' he spat.

'Dunno,' Nosebleed replied, before twirling round to face his new mates. 'How much do they charge for a ride then?'

'Sixty quid, for half an hour. There's a bit of a queue on like, it's heaving in there.'

'Well we can always have a beer while we're waiting, can't we lads?'

'Yeeeaahhh!!!!' the cheer went up.

…

A couple of hours later I saw them pass the window as they returned from Winson's, looking even more tanked than they had when they went over. I quickly hit the deck, before they spotted me and crawled, commando style, to the office door. I pushed it open, crawled through and bolted it behind me again, before standing and watching warily through the peephole.

'That was…fucking shhit,' Rob slurred at his mates. 'A fucking tenner to get in, five quid for a shit beer and a two hour wait for a bird that couldn't even get me hard.'

'Yeah,' Nosebleed agreed with him. 'There was plenty of birds, they just need more rooms.'

'I wanna know where that fucking receptionist is,' Rob scowled staring at the door I was hiding behind. He seemed to be looking straight at me and I gulped, shitting myself that he could tell that I was there.

'Come on Rob you twat,' Nosebleed ordered him. 'If you don't hurry up I'm fucking locking you out of the room.'

Rob just stared at the door malevolently. Even in that state, I was sure the big bastard would get the better of me toe to toe, and I began eying up objects in the room I could barricade myself in the room with.

'You'll save,' he spat at the door. 'You'll fucking save.'

He turned, stumbled through the door and I heard him shouting at his mates to wait for him.

What a cock, I mused. I'd love to have seen him getting his ass kicked by whoever gave him the black eye. Still he had given me an idea with the brothel, not a bad little idea at all.

Chapter 10

Exactly one week later my first pay cheque from the hotel came through the post.

'What the hell is this?' I demanded of a bemused looking Brent from behind his desk as I waved the slip at him.

'It's your payslip,' the sarcastic fuck replied.

'I know it's my payslip, but it's short.'

'Let me see.'

I slapped it on his desk and folded my arms as he scrutinised the slip over the rim of his glasses.

'It's correct,' Brent announced.

'No it is not. That is a cheque for £156.22. I thought I was being paid six pounds an hour.'

'You are.'

'So that makes two hundred and forty pounds a week.'

'Yes it does but obviously we deduct tax and national insurance.'

'Not almost a hundred quid you don't. My other job, sorry my last job, paid two hundred and seventy pounds and yet I still paid less tax than this.'

'Let me have another look,' Brent said, scrutinising the slip again.

'Oh, I see what's wrong here. You are being taxed as though this is a second job. There must have been a mistake at the tax office. Because they think it's your second job you are paying tax on every penny rather than everything you earn above your tax code.'

Shit, of course. Why hadn't I thought of that?

'Do you want me to call the tax office?' Brent offered. 'I can tell them they have made a mistake.'

'Er, no. I think I'll call them myself.'

'Use the phone if you like.'

'No…no thanks. I'll call them later.'

'Well if you're sure.'
'I'm sure, thanks anyway.'

I made my excuses and left. I couldn't very well let Brent know that this was a second job, not after I had told him I was a student at my interview. Questions would be asked.

This would call for a serious re-evaluation of my five month plan. I was now earning a good forty quid a week less than I expected to at the hotel. Over the next five months that would leave me just over a thousand pounds shy of what I had calculated I would save. If the topical treatments failed I would not be able to revert to Plan B and undergo the hair transplants. What's more, the topicals, if I were to persevere with them, were now potentially raping my poor beleaguered wallet to the tune of one hundred and fifty American dollars a month. With my rent, bills and drink habit, that left me very little to play with from my council wage.

Another source of income would have to be found and I knew just the place. I resolved to pay the place a visit the minute my shift ended.

...

'Hello darling,' a chubby faced woman with short ginger hair, greeted me from behind the bars.

'Er, good morning. I'm looking for the proprietor of the establishment.'

'The proprietor eh? Well who's looking for her?'

Her?

'My name's Paul.'

'What you want with her Paul?'

'I have a business proposition.'

'Sorry Paul, it's a straight joint, we don't need any rent boys.'

'I'm not a rent boy, you cheeky bitch. I work in the hotel across the road'

'You look like a rent boy, all skin and bones.'

'Well I'm not OK, now can I please see Winston?'

'Wait here.'

She disappeared from behind the bars and I heard a door open somewhere out of my line of vision. Another door opened at the side of me and the lard mountain that had confused me for a rent boy stood in front of me.

'Are you gonna get the owner for me or not?' I asked.

'I am the owner, sweetcheeks.'

'Oh, what about Winston?'

'There isn't a Winston.'

'So why the hell do you call the place Winson's?'

'Isn't it obvious?'

'No.'

'Well let me ask you a question. When you came over here did you expect to be making a business proposition to a woman?'

'No.'

'No you expected to be talking to a big black man didn't you?'

'Yes.'

'Exactly, and would you call a big black man called Winston a cheeky bitch?'

'Er, no. Sorry about that.'

'Exactly, and as long as drunken punters think there's a Winston on the premises they are less likely to give me any hassle aren't they?'

'So why did you just tell me there wasn't a Winston?'

She looked me up and down, sneering as she did so.

'Let's face it darling; at nine and a half stone or whatever it is you weigh, you're not going to be giving me much trouble are you? Now what's this proposition of yours?'

...

My plan was simple, on Friday and Saturday nights, when the brothel had more customers than rooms, I would rent out one of the hotel's rooms for an arranged rate per hour.

'Ok Paul, that sounds like an interesting plan. But let me just ask you this: Why would I pay you for a room by the hour when I can just book a couple of the rooms for the whole night and use them as a spill-over?'

'Me. I'm to stop you. Let's just say that if I suspected that you *were* doing that I would have the police over in an instant. I'd tell them that I'd heard screaming coming from the room, then let them in, for the occupants own safety, where they would doubtless realise that the local brothel was utilising a reputable hotel. They'd shut you down within a week, our manager would insist upon it.'

She didn't seem to like the threat at all and I was afraid for a moment that the walrus would actually eat me, but her snarl turned into a smile and she eventually replied.

'And how much would you be expecting to charge me, per hour, for the privilege of utilising such a reputable hotel?'

'Twenty pounds an hour?' I replied, more as a question than a demand.

'Fifteen and you've got yourself a deal Paul.'

'Fifteen it is then.'

'And will the rooms be available from tonight?'

'Well I'm not sure about tonight I'll have to find out if the hotel is fully booked first. If it is we will have to start next week. Do you have a telephone number I can contact you on?'

'Yes,' she said scribbling her name and number on a piece of paper.

Monique 0113 2428106

Monique, what a great name for a madame I thought as I read the name and number.

'Now is there anything else I can help you with? You'll appreciate that I am a very busy woman.'

'Er, no. That's all. I'll call you about the rooms tonight.'

I had rather been hoping for a tour of the premises, maybe a freebie from one of the girls, but I didn't want to push my luck just yet. Better to get Monique onside for a few weeks first.

Chapter 11

When I returned home I found a card from the postman informing me that he had called round with a parcel that was too large to fit through the letterbox. I could collect it from the depot after twelve o' clock. The depot closed at twelve thirty on Saturdays so I set my alarm for eleven thirty and had a three hour power nap, before jumping out of bed with the alarm and racing down to the post depot before it closed.

Once there I handed in my card from the mailman and collected my parcel. It was a big one, seemingly with two separate containers inside, which I reasoned must have been the concealing products. I didn't dare open it on the street for fear it had 'Spray on Hair' emblazoned upon the packaging so I rushed home, where upon I ripped open the envelope and held before me one can and one tube of fresh hope.

Any hopes I had for the COUVRé were soon dashed. *It's Hollywood's best kept secret* the literature announced.

'It's brown paint!' I screamed at the mirror as I tried to smudge on the foul smelling paste with the sponge that was supplied.

By eliminating the contrast between your hair and scalp you will immediately see a fuller head of hair.

By painting my bald spot brown I immediately saw a fuller head of paint. Was I seriously expected to make people believe that I wasn't in fact going bald by colouring in the patch? I might as well have spent my money on a brown magic marker. I shampooed the shit out and took another disgusted look at the accompanying pictures. They showed some grey bald guy frowning on one and then the same guy, smiling this time, with a head of hair that would make Slash from Guns and Roses look thin on top.

I looked for the name of the manufacturer on the box so that I might send the crap back to them, complete with letter of complaint. My heart sank as I noted that the manufacturer, Spencer Forrest, was the same one that made Toppik, my other (now very faint) glimmer of hope. I picked up the can of Toppik and tore off the protective plastic that covered it. It looked like a big pepper shaker and I shook it over my hand to look at the fibres that were inside. They were tiny, dust like fibres that it took a good wash to get off my palm. At least it looks like it might stay in, I thought.

I waited for my hair to dry and read the leaflet that came with it in the meantime. There were similar pictures to the grey guy in the COUVRé packaging; bald and frowning before pictures, hairy and smiling after pictures.

You'll be amazed how these Hair Building Fibers transform your thin, colourless 'vellus' hairs. Suddenly, this 'peach fuzz' becomes thick and full before your eyes.

I made the long, drawn out sigh of someone who has just been conned out of a significant amount of money and headed to the bathroom to do the shake and vac on my bald patch.

You apply Toppik by simply holding the custom container over your thinning area, and shaking it gently. In seconds, thousands of tiny colour matched hair fibers will intertwine with your own hair. Charged with static electricity, they bond so securely that they will stay in place all day and night, in even the strongest wind or hardest rain.

I shook for exactly thirty seconds, watching the tiny particles fall from the canister as I did so. I had obviously held it too far from my head because the fucking shit got everywhere: In the sink, the bathroom shelf and all over the shoulders of my white t shirt. I gave the patch a rub, as per the instructions and picked up the vanity mirror more out of duty than hope.

A miracle, the bald spot was gone. Well, technically it was hidden, secreted beneath a coating of shredded sheep's wool (for that is what Toppik is made from), dyed medium brown. I fell to my knees and praised God for giving me back my life and then got up again to admire the rear of my head again in the vanity mirror.

Viva la fucking Toppik.

...

It didn't take long for the religious experience I felt at covering the patch to diminish. I quickly found that despite the claim that it would *bond so securely that they will stay in place all day and night, in even the strongest wind or hardest rain,* that this wasn't exactly true. Wind wasn't really a problem, especially after I started spraying my mane with copious amounts of industrial strength hairspray.

It did however come off quite easily when I rubbed my head, and after I scratched it I would get the particles under my finger nails which made them look like I'd been working down a coal mine. This meant that I had to avoid scratching my head; which ordinarily would have been bad enough but was made worse by the fact that the particles, coupled with the hairspray seemed to irritate my scalp almost as bad as the Minoxidil did before I added Nizoral to my regimen.

But the real enemy was rain. Contrary to the claims made on the packaging, the fibres did not stand up to the hardest rain, nor I found out did they stand up to a light drizzle.

I first discovered the Achilles' heel in Toppik's 'advanced technology' when I was shopping in town. With my newfound confidence I felt like John Travolta in *Saturday Night Fever* as I clicked my fingers and strutted down the high street. You could tell by the way I used my walk I was a woman's man and I admired my flowing locks each time I caught my reflection in the shop windows.

After purchasing some new garments with which to further enhance my appearance I stepped back outside to find that, as is often the case in my accursed country, the weather had decided to take a turn for the worse. Not to worry, I thought, it's only spitting and I set off down the high street clicking my fingers again. The rain became a little heavier and began to run down my face. I wiped my forehead dry with my hand and looked at it afterwards. To my horror, it was covered in what looked like soot. Jesus, what the fuck was happening? I stuck a tentative finger from the other hand onto my patch and then examined it. Sure enough the tip looked was now covered in a wet, black powder.

Hardest rain my arse, you lying bastards. I had to walk home three miles in the rain that day, as I was too embarrassed to get on the bus with my stained forehead and smudgy patch. After this humiliating episode I was careful to always carry a cap with me or wear hooded tops in case of emergency.

But all things considered and with prudent measures like the cap and hooded tops taken into account, I was a very happy customer. I could work at the hotel without my hat on and I knew that when it was time to return to my real job with the council that I could do so with the monk patch buried beneath the Toppik fibres.

Business at the hotel was going well too, I had started booking room sixty nine, which I found highly appropriate, under a false name and paying for it myself.

This cost me fifty pounds a night but I was able to make about seventy five pounds back from Monique's girls during the course of the night. I did this on Saturdays and Sundays which meant fifty quid in cash, almost enough to cover the extra tax I was paying for this being my second job. After a few weeks I expanded the operation to include room seventy as well, which took my level of additional earnings to about a hundred quid for the two nights.

Then I had a stroke of fortune that was to take my ill gotten gains to another level. It was when I started my shift and took over from the Janet creature that worked on reception.

'Hi Paul, I'm gonna have to dash off. I'm supposed to be picking up my boyfriend from the pub in ten minutes,' the hefty lass informed me. 'Oh, before I forget. Room thirty seven is out of order, you mustn't book it out to anyone. The shower is broken.'

I was still reeling from the fact that the ugly hag in front of me actually had a boyfriend when the idea struck me. Of course, why hadn't I thought of this before? The prostitutes didn't really need to use the shower, I could rent this room to them. Not only that but I could deliberately sabotage a different room each week and then use that as the brothel's spill over, thus saving me fifty quid a night in the process.

Genius.

Chapter 12

By now I was building up quite an arsenal of weapons with which to defend my hairline. The extra cash afforded to me by the sabotaging of rooms at the hotel meant that I could stockpile weapons of mass hair-loss reduction such as Minoxidil and Nizoral. I also spent large amounts of money on a range of conventional weapons, such as American Crew Thickening Lotion and Redken Densify.

I decided to invest some of the money in a landline telephone and the internet too, so that I could order my hair products from the comfort of my own home instead of having to make sure no one was peering at my screen in the library.

This gave me the opportunity of lurking on a couple of hair loss forums, where I was able to read other men's tales of misery and self loathing, as well as compare their regimens to my own. Almost the entire online bald community seemed to be on Minoxidil. Nizoral seemed to be a favourite too but there didn't seem to be too many people on the old Crinagen and this was a cause of immense concern to me, though not exactly a great surprise. The fucking stuff stank like rotten eggs, especially if applied directly before or after the Minoxidil. In fact the smell was so repugnant that I took to only applying it before bed and washing my hair as soon as I woke up.

The universal opinion on almost all the independent forums was that Propecia, the potentially impotence inducing tablet, was the only way to block the dreaded DHT. With the Crinagen making my pillow reek like an old hen's fanny, coupled with the fact that it didn't appear to be halting the enemy's advance at all, I knew that eventually I would have to seriously consider the Propecia.

...

Sabotaging rooms at the hotel was a little trickier than I first thought, my chief antagonist was Andy, the maintenance guy. Andy was a nice enough bloke but a pain in the arse for my finances. If I blocked a toilet with a full roll of shit paper, this fucker stuck his arm in and scraped it out again. If I planted a burnt out fuse in the television or kettle or I shorted a light-bulb, Andy would have it replaced by noon.

There was one chink in the hotel's armour however, Andy did not work weekends. That meant that although the hotel would be in full working order on Friday afternoon, it could be successfully sabotaged in time for Saturday night. This meant that I usually had to pay for a couple of rooms myself on Friday, but I made up for it by blocking a toilet and sabotaging a fuse box in time for Saturday. In order to make it look less suspicious I always stuck to the same two rooms, sixty nine (for posterity's sake) got a toilet block and twenty three would suffer constant power surges, wiping out the TV and Kettle. I also endeavoured to make sure that I interfered with the rooms through the week too. Not for financial gain, but to avoid a pattern emerging where the rooms were only faulty on weekends. It had the advantage of making it seem that these rooms were pre-disposed to disorder.

And so I continued with this fantastically fertile method of misappropriation for the next month and a half, seemingly on course for my magic three grand.

Chapter 13

No one would have believed as they rode the number ninety two bus to Leeds that their hairlines were being watched keenly and closely from the back of the bus by a man with fewer follicles than their own; that as these men busied themselves about their various concerns they were being scrutinised and studied, perhaps almost as narrowly as a man with a microscope might scrutinise the transient creatures that swarm and multiply in a drop of water. With infinite complacency the men boarded and alighted before going about their little affairs, serene in their assurance of hair atop of their heads. Yet from the back of the bus, I regarded their mullets, short-back and sides and partings with envious eyes, and slowly but surely I drew my plans to join them.

In town I alighted the ninety two and headed in the direction of The Mixing Tin. As I did so I continued to scrutinize each and every male hairline I walked behind. I was amazed at how many balding men there were; perhaps one in every four. Twenty five percent of the adult male population appeared to be thinning! Where was the government aid? I could imagine the amount of man hours that were lost to depression brought on by impending baldness, it must run into the millions. The real injustice to me was that almost every tramp I passed, and there are plenty of them in Leeds, had a full (albeit greasy and matted) head of the stuff. How? Was it the cider?

Amazingly *some* of the bald men I walked behind were laughing and seemingly enjoying life. Even more astonishing still, others were accompanied by beautiful women, arm in arm! They didn't seem to be at all bothered about their condition. But the vast majority had a despondent look about them. They trudged rather than walked, with their heads bowed, limp arms carried heavily, zombie like, resigned to a life of ridicule and derision. It was too depressing, I needed a drink. The Mixing Tin beckoned.

'Afternoon Marty,' I saluted the innkeeper.

'Alright mate,' he replied, peeling himself from the only other punter in the place, a rather attractive looking young maiden with curly brown hair, a bit of a Minnie Driver look-alike. 'Pint of cider is it?'

'Yep.'

I took my drink and retreated to the back of the empty bar.

'You not joining us?' the Minnie Driver look-alike called over.

'Err…'

'Come on sweetheart, park your ass up here, next to me.'

I looked at Marty, he didn't seem very keen on me joining the party and I didn't really want to be stepping on his toes.

'You coming or what?' she asked again. 'Tell him to come over Marty.'

'Come over,' he said dutifully.

'Err, OK,' I replied, picking myself up and moving over to the bar.

'What's your name then?' Minnie asked.

'Paul.'

'Aren't you gonna ask me mine?'

'What's your name?' I asked.

'Guess.'

'I don't know.'

'Guess.'

'Minnie?'

'Why Minnie?'

'I don't know, you look a bit like Minnie Driver I guess.'

'Do I really?' she gasped. 'Oh my God, that's so kind of you.'
'So what's your real name?'
'Rebecca.'
'It's a nice name, same as my mums.'
'That's funny, my dad's called Paul.'
'Really?'
'No, not really. Had you going though didn't I?'
'I guess you did.'
'You gonna buy a girl a drink are you Paul?'
So that's what she was after.
'OK, what you want?'
'Three Jagermeisters.'
'Three?'
'Yep, one for me, one for you and one for Marty.'
'OK, three Jagermeisters please Marty.'

…

Rebecca and I sat drinking for the next three hours while Marty scowled behind the bar. His mood worsened as we got more and more drunk and eventually he cut Rebecca off, refusing to serve her any more alcohol. She wasn't really that drunk, just loud, but Marty had been gazumped by one of his punters and he wasn't happy.
'Fair enough,' she slurred. 'I'll take my business elsewhere. Come on Paul darling.'
'…'
'Come on sweetheart, we'll get something to eat.'
'Where?'
'I don't know, you choose.'
I looked at Marty apologetically. He shrugged as if he didn't care what I did, but his eyes betrayed his frustration.
'Err, OK. How about Thai Edge?'

'That wouldn't be a Thai place by any chance?'
'Yes.'
'They sell beer there?'
'Yeah, course they sell beer.'
'Then let's go honey,' she hollered, wrapping her arm around me.

We climbed the stairs from The Mixing Tin into the cold air outside. It was still light and the streets were busy.

'You'll have to excuse my ignorance; I haven't graced a Thai restaurant for a while, do you think they'll serve vegetarian fare?'
'I should think so. You're a veggie are you?'
'I sure am sweetheart.'
'Save the animals eh?'
'Not really, I don't do moral crusading. Quite frankly I just don't like the texture, it's disgusting. Chicken skin in particular makes me want to vomit, how can people actually eat that stuff. Have you seriously sat down and thought about it? A *chicken's skin*, for God's sakes.'
'You're starting to put me off the stuff.'
'Wise men outlive carnivores dearest.'
'So you're not one of those so called veggies that eat fish then?'
'I haven't eaten any animal since I was twelve years old. I did have to pretend to be an animal lover at first, it was the only way I could get my parents to stop force feeding me the filthy stuff. It's funny really, back then people forced their children to eat *all* their meat because it was the most expensive part of the meal. These days they try to make them eat *all* their vegetables for the exact same reason.'
'As long as you're not going to resent me for tucking into mine.'

'As I said, I'm no crusader. In fact the moral vegetarians make me sick. It's funny when you meet another vegetarian, they immediately assume that you are a save the animals type, just like them. One girl in particular at university used to keep inviting me to these bloody M*eat Is Murder* demonstrations she used to attend. She would drone on and on for hours about the whole thing. In the end I had to tell her to shut the fuck up and that I wasn't interested in the God damned animals. In fact the animals could go fuck themselves. I actually told her that I intended to renounce my vegetarianism, because I didn't want people to associate me with people like her. She hasn't spoken to me since, but then I'm good at that, pissing off casual acquaintances with my outspoken views.'

'Well I think you're wonderful.'

'Thank you sweetheart. I think you're wonderful too.'

Chapter 14

The sound of an unfamiliar alarm roused me. Then footsteps and the sound of a shower running in the next room. I tentatively opened one eye and realised I was not in my own bed. My God, I had actually scored. My mind replayed images of Rebecca kissing me while attempting to run her fingers through my hair. I recalled flinching, to protect the Toppik from coming off on her hands. I looked at the pillow, it was a white one. Shit. A black imprint from the back of my head was imprinted on it, like a smaller version of the Turin Shroud. Bloody white pillows. I rubbed it against the blue quilt and it faded slightly. The shower stopped in the other room.

'You'll have to get up in a minute,' Rebecca shouted from the bathroom. 'I have to work at nine.'

'OK,' I replied.

I jumped up pulled on my pants and top and frantically scanned the room for my rucksack. There it was, right next to the bedroom door. I grabbed the bag and ripped it open, rummaging around for the trucker cap I kept in case of rain.

'You ready?' Rebecca said as the bedroom door began to open.

'Not yet,' I replied jamming my foot into it to prevent her entering.

'Hey, what you playing at?'

'Sorry, I'm not fully dressed yet.'

'So?'

'So I'm shy.' I had my back holding the door closed now.

'You weren't shy last night.'

'Well I am now. Can I just have a minute please?'

'Fair enough, be a prude. But I like a man who's comfortable with his body.' She let go of the handle and allowed me to close the door properly.

You're with the wrong guy here, I thought.

'I am, it's just that I'm still a bit...you know...excited...I didn't want to freak you out.'

'Really? You are a horny devil, but what makes you think it would freak me out?'

'I don't know,' I replied, unzipping and re-zipping my pants to make it sound like I was getting dressed. I plonked the cap on my head and opened the door. Rebecca stood before me, one towel round her body and one wrapped round her head. I could smell the fresh scent of the shower gel, she looked gorgeous.

'I'd give you a blowjob,' she said. 'But I'm late for work as it is. Do you want to meet up tonight?'

'I'm supposed to be working.'

'Working? On a Friday night?'

'Yeah, I work as a night porter at a hotel in town.'

'I thought you worked for the council?'

'I do,' I replied, wondering at what point I had told her that. 'It's kind of a long story. I've been on long term sick and working at the hotel in the meantime.'

'On the sick? What's wrong with you?'

'I can't say.'

'Very secretive today aren't you?'

'Not really, I just don't want you to think any less of me.'

'I wouldn't think any less of you sweetie. Besides, it can't be that bad if you are managing to work at the hotel.'

'It's nothing really, but the council gives you up to six months sick on full pay, so I might as well take advantage eh?'

'So that's where my council tax goes eh? Paying malingering employee's wages?'

'I'll make it up to you. What time do you finish work? I can take you out for dinner before I start at the hotel. Pay you some of that council tax back.'
'Yes I think I'll let you do that. I finish at five thirty.'
'OK, and where did you say you work again?'
'You don't remember?'
'Well we were a little drunk. At least I can remember your name.'
'What is it?'
'Rebecca.'
'Fair enough, I work part time at the Job Centre.'
'Of course, how could I forget?'
'Yeah, so if you plan to go on the sick from the hotel as well, maybe I can help you find a third job.'
'Two's more than enough for now thanks. Besides I don't think the hotel pay sickness benefit.'
'Come on then dear, it's time I got myself to work.'
We rode the bus together to town. It was chock full of schoolchildren; screaming, pimple faced brats throwing things around the bus. The driver chastised them a few times, but they carried on regardless. I narrowly missed being struck by flying pencils on a number of occasions.
'Shit, do you ride this bus all the time?' I asked her.
'Only if I miss the eight o' clock bus, which for obvious reasons I try not to do.'
'Yeah, I can see why. This is not what you need when you're nursing a hangover.'
'You're right about that sweetie. But I try to get through the whole ordeal by guessing what some of the children might be when they grow up.'
'Convicts, most of these fuckers,' I replied as another pencil flew past my head.
'No doubt some of them will be, that fat one at the front pushing the skinny Chinese kid around, he looks like he'll

end up behind bars. As for the Chinese kid he's tormenting, I reckon he'll be a police officer when he grows up.'

'What makes you say that?'

'I don't know; the bullying perhaps? Sometimes people who are bullied at school want to get even in adulthood. A police officer is an ideal way to do that. He'll be motivated by memories of the laughing, taunting faces from school and will subsequently become an exceptional officer, rapidly progressing through the ranks. He'll be an inspector by the time he's thirty, you mark my words.'

'What about the ginger kid sat at the front?'

'Suicide case.'

'What?'

'Suicide case, he'll most likely hang himself.'

'Why?'

'Well for a start he's ginger, that's bound to be the root of an unhappy childhood, especially if he has a stepfather.'

'What difference does that make?'

'Have you never heard the expression *beaten like a ginger stepchild*?'

'No.'

'Oh. Anyway years of being abused by his stepfather will make him hand shy, so becoming a police officer is right out for him. He may struggle in a few menial jobs until he gets to his mid twenties, which is when that pronounced crown that he is currently sporting turns out to be a bald patch, do you see it?'

'…'

'What's wrong?'

'Er, nothing. Sorry. Do carry on.'

'Are you OK? You look a bit pale.'

'No, I'm fine. Just a bit hung over I guess. You were saying?'

'Where was I? Oh yes the bald patch. Well for him the emasculating march towards mutilating baldness may actually be a relief at first. As his scalp rids itself of the genetic flaw that has cursed him since birth he will be elated, only to discover that fate has a sting in its tail. Only the hair on the top of his head will fall out, the sides and back will remain as hairy and ginger as they have always been. Half bald, half ginger, what a cruel, cruel fate that would be. Suicide seems to be the natural conclusion.'

'...'

'Are you sure you are OK?'

'No, I think I'm going to be sick.'

'Shit, you'd better get off the bus.'

'I think I need to, sorry. It's the hangover.'

'I can't get off with you, I need to get to work.'

'That's alright, I'll call you about tonight. I better go, I don't feel well at all.'

'You poor thing, see you tonight.'

'Yeah see you,' I replied scrambling through the horde of brats on the bus.

I alighted at the next stop and stuck my head over the refuse bin, vomiting as I did so. I held my head in there for about five minutes, my stomach churning, my throat aching from retching repeatedly and my mind remorselessly replaying the same two words.

Mutilating baldness.

Chapter 15

Once home again, I fired the PC up and logged onto the net. First stop, *Hairlosstalk.com*. Select Topic, hmm, should I choose S*hedding, Shedding, Shedding, Success Stories* or *Tell Your Story?* I think we'll go for S*uccess Stories*. I opened the link and clicked onto the first story that caught my eye; *Re-growing On Propecia (pics included)*.

Hi guys,

First of all, let me say that I had absolutely NO side effects from the Propecia whatsoever. If anything my sexual appetite has INCREASED since I added this wonder drug to my regimen!!! But then again, maybe that's down to the fact that I am dating again!!! After years of hiding under various concealers and hair systems I finally have my own freaking hair back!!! Can you fucking believe it!!! I cannot recommend this shit enough. Take the plunge, believe me. Providing you are not one of the two percent of users who loose the ability to get a boner, you will never regret adding Propecia to your regimen. Check out the pics.

Brian1975

I checked out the pics. They were amazing: Brian, two years ago, looking like Kojak on chemotherapy... eighteen months ago, a few wispy strands of white-ish hair protruding from his cranium...twelve months ago, darker hairs... six months, more dark hairs... last month looking like fucking David Beckham (albeit an *ugly* David Beckham).
Jesus.

I checked out Brian's Hairlosstalk credentials; Senior Poster, over a thousand posts. I clicked on the link marked Read All User's Posts and read a number of them to satisfy myself that he wasn't some guy who was there to promote a certain drug or clinic. He evidently wasn't, judging by the range of products that he had experimented with and the hope and money he had invested in each of these snake oils. I read his current regimen which consisted of Minoxidil, Nizoral and Propecia.

The Big Three.

I then browsed a number of other S*uccess Stories* and inspected the regimen that these lucky bastards had used. Every last one of them was on the Propecia. I couldn't find a single person that was cheering Crinagen on, not fucking one. In fact the only people using Crinagen seemed to be the ones that were too afraid to try Propecia or the ones that had suffered a limp dick from it. It seemed obvious to me then, I had been wasting my time with the stuff. If I was going to re-grow my own hair and avoid the need to sprinkle Toppik on at regular intervals I would need to introduce the big guns to the armoury. Victory through superior firepower.

...

Rebecca sent me an SMS at three o'clock.

'Hi Swt thing, r we stll meeting 2nite? Hope so, c u later xxx R.'

I sent a reply saying yes, I would meet her outside The Mixing Tin at five thirty. She sent another, saying that was great, but could we not eat there, she would choose tonight. No problem, I told her, that saved me having to think of somewhere impressive.

…

'Sorry I'm late sweetie,' Rebecca apologised, playing innocently with a lock of her curly brown hair.

'No problem, it's only ten minutes.'

'I got held up by the boss, she wants me to work more hours, go full time.'

'Is that good?'

'Hell no, that's not good. Do you realise how depressing it is working in the Job Centre? How much abuse I take on a daily basis from people blaming me personally for the fact that their social security cheque hasn't arrived or the fact that they are ineligible for benefits because they have savings in the bank. *I've paid into the system all my life*, they scream at me. *And now, when I need benefits YOU tell me I am not entitled because I have savings in the bank*. I try to explain to them, *I don't make the rules*, but they don't care, they just need someone to shout at. Some of the staff have actually been assaulted in the past.'

'Jesus.'

'Yeah, fortunately I haven't been attacked yet, but I'm sure it's only a matter of time. I have a way of winding people up, as I already told you.'

'Yeah, you did mention that,' I replied, thinking about her 'mutilating baldness' remark that afternoon. 'So where are we eating anyway?'

'I was thinking of eating at the Iranian café behind the Corn Exchange.'

'Iranian?'

'Yes Iranian.'

'Do they serve vegetarian food there?'

'Of course, they do excellent roast pepper and goats cheese sandwiches.'

'Do they, er…'

'Serve meat?'

I was thinking of booze actually, but didn't want to sound like an alcoholic.

'Yes, serve meat, it's just that...' I began to say instead.

'Don't worry sweetie. I've told you, eat what you like, I don't care.'

'Sorry.'

'Don't be sorry, just take me for dinner. I'm starving.'

It took five minutes to stroll to the Iranian café, during which time Rebecca complained about her part time job and the stresses of working and being a student at the same time. I had forgotten all about her being a student, and had to skilfully extract the nature of her studies from her once again without being accused of having not listened the night before. She studied Fine Art.

I had never had Iranian food and had to rely on Rebecca to suggest something, which turned out to be less exotic than I had expected. It was basically a chicken, cheese and humus sandwich, served in a type of flat bread. Unfortunately, but not unsurprisingly there was no booze on the menu, so I had to settle for sipping a mint tea. Refreshing, but not exactly what I'd had in mind. We sat on great big cushions on the floor and I surveyed the room. I had expected the place to be full of Arabs and Persians, but it was predominantly young, white student types, all of whom were sucking on shisha pipes. The room smelled of apple tobacco, really quite pleasant.

'Rebecca.'

'Yes?'

'Do you mind if I ask you why you ended up pulling me last night?'

'So I pulled you did I?'

'Well yes. *You* called *me* over to have a drink with you, *you* insisted we went for dinner and then *you* took me back to your apartment.'

'OK, OK, don't make me sound desperate.'

'I don't think you're desperate, it's just that I can't understand why you ended up pulling me. Especially as you were already with Marty at the bar. Let's face it he's a lot better looking than me.'

'Is he?'

'I think that's fairly evident, believe me hundreds of girls would testify to that.'

'Well I'm not hundreds of girls am I? In fact I found Marty to be extremely unattractive. Good for a laugh I suppose, but not exactly my type.'

'Why not?'

'Too pretty.'

'Eh?'

'He's too well groomed. I mean I like a man to be clean and tidy as much as the next girl, but when he's spending longer in the bathroom than I am it's a little off putting.'

'What makes you think he spends all his time in the bathroom?'

'Oh please. Have you honestly never noticed that he plucks his eyebrows?'

'No.'

'Well he does. Nobody's eyebrows are that uniform believe me. Then there's the fake tan, the waxed chest and the trendy haircut that no doubt takes him half an hour to fine-tune. The man is vanity personified, I guarantee there are love bites on his mirror.'

'Wow, you have an eye for detail,' I remarked, a little worriedly. Had she noticed the Toppik?

'I notice things.'

'So what did you like about me?'

'I don't know, I liked the fact that you didn't mind sitting in the bar by yourself. Most young men wouldn't dream of going to the pub by themselves, they usually drink in packs, confusing their loudness for being funny. You must have noticed how loudly these types laugh at their own jokes? The cocky air of confidence they exude is a sham, derived entirely from the drink and the fact they are surrounded by their mates. Put any one of them in a pub by themselves and they shut the fuck up, but in a pack seemingly normal people behave like fucking yobs. I liked the fact that you were confident enough to sit in the bar by yourself.'

'So were you.'

'Yes, you're right, but it's a little different. As a reasonably attractive woman I can expect men to gravitate towards me. Marty for instance, was in there like a rat up a drainpipe. I am never really short of company, unless I want to be. That does provide a different problem however, that of unwanted attention, but I'm strong enough a personality to tell them when their attentions are unrequited. A simple *fuck off* usually does the trick.'

'So you liked the fact that I am a Billy no mates, who doesn't take care of his appearance?'

'No I liked the fact that you are a good looking lad, who doesn't try too hard.'

She might think differently if she knew how long I actually spent with my mirrors aligned on the back of my head, I mused. Indeed I probably spent more time on my hair than Marty did, but for now I was lapping up the fact that she had just referred to me as good looking and confident. I liked the confident bit most of all because it was the diametric opposite of how I viewed myself.

We spent the next two hours eating our food, drinking mint tea and smoking apple shisha. I had honestly never felt as relaxed with a new woman without the aid of alcohol in my life. The conversation flowed easily and if I ran out of things to say, I could just sit back and listen to Rebecca's rants.

'What time do you start at the hotel?' Rebecca asked me glancing at the Persian clock that hung from the wall.

'Ten o' clock.'

'It's eight o' clock now. What shall we do for two hours?'

'I don't know, you don't have to stay out on my behalf. Feel free to go home if you are tired.'

'Who said anything about tired? I'm feeling horny.'

'Really?'

'Really. How much money have you got?'

'In cash, twenty quid.'

'Good, enough for a taxi to my place and back to town. Fancy it?'

'Fancy what?'

'Don't play stupid, you know what. Come on, we can be at mine in twenty minutes, that gives us an hour before you get a taxi back to work.'

…

I worked with a smile on my face that night, in fact I was so busy reminiscing about the amazing hour I had just spent at Rebecca's that I almost, *almost* forgot to sabotage a couple of rooms for the next day. I only remembered when one of the early birds checking out of the hotel informed me that the window in his room would not shut properly. That was at half past five.

'OK sir, thanks. I'll get that sorted this weekend,' I informed him.

When he was out of sight I grabbed a key that had been handed in by another early check out, room twenty four, ran up there and busied myself stuffing as much toilet roll as I could fit down the bowl. There was no time to interfere with a second room but the faulty window that had just been reported might be a good enough reason to put room forty seven out of operation for the night.

Janet came in late at ten past six, apologising for keeping me back.

'Sorry Paul, my car wouldn't start. I had to get my boyfriend to give me a lift. He wasn't very happy about being woken up at five thirty in the morning.'

No I imagine having an ogre like that shaking you awake at anytime must be a fairly traumatic experience.

'Fair enough Janet. Oh, before I go, a guest from room forty seven complained that his window wasn't shutting properly.'

'OK Paul, I'll log it and let Brent know when he comes in.'

'Cheers Janet.'

I didn't mention the blocked toilet. Better to let the cleaners report it, after all it might look suspicious if I was reporting the same types of problem every week.

Chapter 16

The next night I arrived for work at ten o' clock, to be informed by a receptionist called Donna that two rooms were out of order for the evening, forty seven and twenty four.

Perfect.

'OK thanks for letting me know Donna. What you doing with the rest of your night anyway?'

'Nothing much, I'll probably open a bottle of wine and put my feet up.'

'Sounds cosy,' I said as I watched her putting on her coat and heading for the door. 'I wish I was watching TV with a drink and putting my feet up.'

'Oh well Paul, I'll be thinking of you when I pour the first glass,' she replied as she exited.

'Lucky thing,' I shouted and watched her climb into her car. She smiled, waved and then made a drinking motion with her hand before firing up the engine and pulling away.

When she was safely out of sight I opened my bag, took out my pocket TV and a can of cider, cracked open the can and put my feet up in front of the TV. I did, of course, take the precaution of pouring the cider into a styrofoam Pepsi cup and disposing of the can.

Better safe than sorry.

…

At eleven thirty the first of the girls arrived from Winston's. I recognised her as a girl called Mai Lee or something. She was a pretty little South East Asian, possibly Thai. Accompanying her there was a middle aged chap, about forty, balding and dressed in jeans and a checked shirt.

'Hello, I have room book under name of Lee,' Mai informed me, acting the part of a respectable hotel guest, more for the punter's sake than anything else. Not that the silly bastard could possibly expect me to believe that they were genuine lovers, but it was important that I pretended I did not know that anything untoward was going on. It wouldn't do to have people knowing that the night porter was running a brothel in the hotel.

'Oh yes, Miss Lee,' I replied, jabbing away at the keyboard and staring at my computer screen. 'You are in room forty seven. I must warn you however that there is a faulty window in the room, it will not lock properly. Will that be a problem?'

'No it won't,' Bald interjected, obviously keen not to let anything get in the way of him slamming Miss Lee.

'OK sir, here's your key.'

'Thank you.'

'You're welcome,' I replied ogling Mai Lee's unbelievable ass and legs as she led him out of reception towards the rooms. If I ever did manage to get a freebie, I thought, I'd definitely go for Mai Lee.

…

They'd been up there for about half an hour when I heard the sound of the outside door opening. I placed my drink aside, and looked up from my pocket TV.

Shit it was Andy, the maintenance guy, with some stunner I didn't recognise.

'Hello mate,' he greeted me.

'Hello Andy,' I replied, shitting myself. My first thought was that the stunner that he had in tow was one of the girls from Winston's and that he had somehow stumbled upon my sideline. 'What can I do for you Andy?'

'Brent said I could use room forty seven tonight, we've been on a night out in town and we live about thirty miles away. He said if I fixed the window tomorrow I could use the room free tonight.'

'Oh,' I said, looking confused. 'Nobody said anything to me.'

'Well phone Brent if you don't believe me.'

'I'm not saying I don't believe you, it's just that I don't want to get into trouble. Maybe I should phone him to confirm that it's OK. You don't mind waiting a minute do you?'

'Not at all.'

I picked up the phone and thought about punching in my home number and pretending that I had tried to call Brent. I could tell Andy that I couldn't get through to him. No, that wouldn't work, Andy might find out from Brent that I had *not* tried to call him after all. Questions might be asked. I dialled Brent's cell phone number and prayed that he was asleep or it was turned off.

'Hello, Brent speaking,' he answered on the second ring. Fuck!

'Hi Brent, it's Paul. Sorry to disturb you but Andy is here with his girlfriend and he says you have OK'd him to use one of the broken rooms for the night.'

'Yes, that's fine. He's going to fix that room and room twenty four tomorrow morning for me. That way all the rooms will be available for tomorrow night.'

'Er, OK. Just thought I'd better check.'

'No problem, bye.'

'Bye.'

'Everything's OK?' Andy asked.

'Er, yes everything's fine,' I replied rummaging through the drawer where we kept keys for rooms that were out of order and other miscellaneous items. 'Hmm...I...I can't seem to find the key for room forty seven...I...I might have to give you room twenty four instead.'

'No way mate; the toilet's blocked in that one.'

'You can use the toilet down here.'

'Fuck that, we've been drinking. Chances are we'll need the toilet a few times tonight and there's no way we're traipsing down here all night.'

'Well you could fix it now.'

'Bollocks to that pal, I want room forty seven.'

'I'll just have another look.'

I began to rummage through the drawer again. Andy leaned over the counter to watch me as I did so.

'So that's what you get up to all night is it?' he said in an accusing tone.

'What?'

'Watching TV,' he replied, pointing at my pocket TV.

'Oh, oh yes. Only while it's quiet though; I still do all the car park and fire checks.'

'Yeah, sure you do.' He was smiling, but there was sinister look on his face. I hoped it was just the beer, but somehow it felt like Andy had one over me now.

'Is that it there?' Andy asked.

'No that's room twenty four's. Are you sure you don't wa...'

I was stopped in my tracks by the sight of Mai Lee and the bald guy opening the door to reception. Their transient liaison had obviously been a lot briefer than expected. Fuck. But at least Mai Lee would be keeping the key for the next girl to come across with, so I wouldn't have to worry about her slamming it on the desk in front of Andy.

Andy looked across at them as they walked into the reception area. They looked an odd couple, a stunning Asian babe with a bald, middle aged, white man. This obviously wasn't lost on Andy either. He smirked knowingly, obviously surmising that she was his mail order bride. I looked at them too, smiling at first, then grimacing as I realised that Mai Lee did not have the key in her hand. The punter was swinging it angrily as he approached the desk.

'We have decided,' he said, 'to take our business elsewhere. That room is freezing, thanks to the broken window. I would like a full refund thank you.'

'Er, sorry sir. I did warn you about it.'

'Well I had expected the heating to be able to compensate for the open window, but believe me *that* room is Baltic.'

'I can only apologise sir,' I replied, glancing past Bald, Andy and his girlfriend and frowning at Mai Lee, who shrugged her shoulders and mouthed 'sorry'.

'You can apologise yes, but you can also issue a full refund too.'

'I'll do that sir, right away.'

I counted out the cash and handed it back to him as I did so. He then passed it onto Mai Lee, who put it in her purse and winked at me. No doubt to signal that she would return it to me via the next girl. I could see what had happened, Bald had probably been trying to appear chivalrous, getting Mai Lee a refund on her outlay, while also giving me the appearance that they *were* respectable punters. He had no idea that I knew what was going on and this whole episode wouldn't have been a problem at all if Andy hadn't been stood at the counter when it happened. He said nothing until Mai Lee and the bald cunt had left, after which he turned to me with a knowing look.

'So what's going on here then?'

...

I somehow knew that I hadn't heard the last of this from Andy, despite the fact that I fobbed him off with the excuse that I had sold the room without realising it was out of order. Worse still my night's earnings had been slashed in half by the loss of room forty seven to Andy and his girlfriend. This was compounded by an angry Monique who called me at five in the morning demanding to know what had happened to the second room her girls were supposed to be using as an overspill.

'Look Monique,' I screamed back at her, 'why don't you ask fucking Mai Lee what happened to the second room? It was her punter that started kicking off in front off another employee from the hotel. Why did she let him do that? If you're gonna scream and ball at someone, do it to her. I'm gonna have enough shit on my plate making sure I don't get fired for running a brothel over here.'

'Well don't let it happen again, I had a lot of disappointed customers here last night. If that shit happens again I might have to come to an arrangement with another hotel.'

'It won't happen again, just don't blame me for last night. That was a freak incident and, as long as I don't get fired, I'll make sure it doesn't happen again.'

'Well it better not,' the fat bitch snapped, before hanging up.

Just great, Monique was making threats and I was still unsure whether Andy would say anything to Brent. I left the hotel not knowing if I would ever be back. If Andy had rumbled me and said anything to Brent I was sure to get the chop. I decided to text Rebecca, just to say that I'd had a good time on Friday and that I looked forward to seeing her again soon. To my great surprise she texted straight back, saying she had a good time too, and if I wasn't too tired after work would I like to come round now.

There were no buses at six o' clock on a Sunday morning, but I was more than willing to stump up a cab fare to climb into bed with Rebecca. I returned to the hotel and called myself a cab. While waiting for it to arrive I took a trip to the bathroom and pulled the vanity mirror, Toppik and hairspray from my bag. It took about thirty seconds to retouch the patch and I marvelled again at the product that had transformed my life and self image.

By half past six I was cuddled up in bed with Rebecca, she was still half asleep and told me she wasn't in the mood for sex *yet*.

'Did you have a good night at work?' she asked.
'Not really.'
'Why not?'
'It's complicated.'
'How?'
'It just is.'
'What is it with you?'
'I don't understand.'
'You seem so open and tactile one minute, then you get all weird and surreptitious the next.'
'Weird?'
'Yes weird. Preventing me getting in my own room, jumping off the bus to get away from me, now refusing to tell me what happened at work. If you have a wife or girlfriend I would prefer if you told me now.'
'What makes you think I've got a wife?'
'I don't think that, but when you jumped off the bus the other day it did seem a little strange. You were fine one minute, then you just changed. I thought you had either been seen, or didn't want to be seen by someone.'
'No…no it's nothing like that.'

'Then what? What is it?'
'Nothing.'
'Bullshit nothing.'
'Rebecca please believe me I don't have another woman. I'm just a bit weird that's all.'
'You certainly are.'
'Hey, you're not exactly normal either.'
'What constitutes normal?' Rebecca asked sitting up.
'I'm not sure.'
'So what about me do you find abnormal?'
'I don't know, I just said it to take the subject off me.'
'If there is such a thing as normal, I wouldn't want to be it anyway. Normal sounds like boring to me.'
'So it's good that I'm a bit weird then?'
'I suppose so, except for your weird penis.'
'What?'
'I'm joking you idiot, but you should have seen your face. My God, why is it that men are so hung up about their penis? Is it too small? Too thin? Too bendy? Too straight? You really are shallow creatures you know that?'
'Well you could say the same about women, always worrying that their ass looks too big.'
'Yes but that's different, we could do something about our asses if we really wanted. We could diet, or exercise. There's nothing you can do about your penis, you get what you are given and just have to accept it.'
'Not really, there's always the option of a penis enlargement.'
'Does that really work?'
'Of course.'
'How do you know? Have you been looking into it?'
'No!'
'Ooh, getting defensive are we?'

'No, I just know it works. I saw a programme on TV about that guy, whose wife hacked off his dick. He had to have it stitched back on again but later went for a penis enlargement. Apparently it worked and he made a career for himself in the porn industry.'

'Sounds good.'

'What working in the porn industry or chopping off someone's penis?'

'The programme you idiot.'

'Right that's the second time you've called me an idiot this morning. I'm not gonna stand for that anymore,' I said climbing on top of her and tickling her ribs.

'Agghhrr stop, I'm sorry…stop. Please.'

'OK, but you stop calling me an idiot.' I stopped and kissed her on the forehead.

'You're not an idiot.'

'Thank you.'

'It feels like someone here is having penis enlargement,' Rebecca noted, lightly brushing my semi erection until it became solid. I kissed her and she returned it passionately.

'Is my dick *really* weird?' I asked.

'No it's lovely.'

'So are you.'

'Don't be cheesy, just make love to me.'

'Have you got any condoms?'

'No, but it doesn't matter.'

'Are you sure?'

'Yes, come on, I'm really horny…oohh.'

'…'

'…'

'…'

'Paul?'

'Yes?'

'Can we do it in the shower?'

'Do I smell?'

'A little, but it doesn't bother me. I just like sex in the shower.'

'Later then.'

'Why not now?'

Because I'm currently wearing about half an ounce of dyed sheep's wool in my hair to cover up a bald patch you silly bitch.

'I just want to do it here, that's all.'

'You're boring.'

'I told you not to call me boring,' I said quickening my pace.

'Agghhrr…no, you said…uh…not to…call you an…aah…an idiot.'

'Jesus...ohh…fuck.'

'…'

'Shit!'

'…'

'Sorry.'

'It doesn't matter.'

'I think it's because I wasn't wearing a condom.'

'I told you it doesn't matter.'

'Would you like me to kiss you…down there?'

'Later. In the shower.'

Fuck.

Chapter 17

I woke to the sound of the TV being put on in the bedroom.

'Wake up lazy,' Rebecca whispered.

'Uh, lazy? I was working until six in the morning. What time is it now?'

'Two in the afternoon.'

'Oh, have you cooked me some breakfast?'

'Cheeky bastard, no I haven't.'

'You're not much of a host are you?'

'I guess not, I was kind of hoping you were hungry for something else.'

'Hey, I'm always hungry for something else.'

'Come on then, I've run a bath. We can get in it together.'

'Er, are you sure we will both fit in?'

'Of course we will, you're not exactly Arnold Schwarzenegger you know.'

'I'm not sure I really want a bath.'

'There you go again, being weird. I think I know what's wrong with you.'

'You do?'

'Yes, you're embarrassed about your body aren't you?'

'Am I?'

I guess I was in a way, but that wasn't the reason I didn't want to get in the bath with her.

'Yes, that's why you wouldn't let me get in my own room after the first night we spent together and that's why you won't get in the bath or shower with me. I'm right aren't I?'

'OK you got me,' I replied, thinking quickly. 'It's my chicken legs I suppose. They resemble something you might find hanging out of a crow's nest.'

'Well, there's nothing to be ashamed of, I like skinny blokes. Come on let's get in the bath.'

'OK.'

I reluctantly climbed out of bed and stood naked in front of her. I looked down at my scrawny frame and shrivelled dick and held out my arms. It wasn't a pretty sight, not even to its owner.

'See, you don't have to hide yourself from me,' Rebecca said, smiling.

'So how come you still get to wear clothes?'

'Would you rather I didn't?'

'Of course.'

I could feel the blood rushing to my dick as she disrobed in front of me. She had a handsome figure alright, all curves but not at all fat. Jesus what did this woman see in me? I motioned toward her and she took hold of my erection in her hand. We kissed for a while before Rebecca began to lead me into the bathroom by my dick while looking over her shoulder at me, like she was walking the dog or something.

'Rebecca?'

'Yes sweetie.'

'Can I have a minute in the bathroom first?'

'Of course you can. Shout me when you're ready.'

'Thanks.'

I closed the bathroom door and listened to make sure she wasn't still standing outside. I heard her moving into the bedroom, singing some Bob Marley song or another; I think it was *Three Little Birds*. I frantically searched the bathroom for a vanity mirror that I could check on the state of yesterday's Toppik with. There wasn't one. What fucking woman in the world didn't have a vanity mirror in her bathroom? The odds on that were astronomical. I tried to tilt my head so that I could see the back of it in the mirror but it was no good, so I licked a finger and stuck it in the general area of the patch and then inspected the finger. There was some black powder on there, but not much. Most have it must have rubbed off on her pillows. I flushed the toilet and washed the powder from my finger before climbing into the bath, with the taps in my back so that when she came in she would see me from the front.

'Ready Rebecca,' I shouted.

'Coming.'

She walked into the bathroom and I felt myself stirring under the water at the sight of her again.

'Ah, you gave yourself the side with the taps. You're such a gentleman aren't you?'

'I guess I am. The water's nice, just the right temperature.'

'Do you want me to wash your back?' she asked.

'No! Er, no. Just get in here with me will you, I'll wash yours.'

…

I made up for my earlier disaster between the sheets by lasting a lot longer in the bath. The fact that I was concentrating so much on the simultaneous acts of penetrating her, stroking her clitoris with my finger, attempting to hide my crown *and* stop her stroking my head meant that I was too pre-occupied to properly enjoy the experience. I could have gone on for months. When she eventually came, she tried to pull me close to her to hug me. Conscious of the fact that this would give her an up close view of my re-emerging tonsure, I resisted this with all my might but my knees were slipping in the bath. We were in some sort of affectionate tug of war, and she was winning.

'Rebecca, you're going to hurt us.'
'Just give me a hug.'
'Let me climb behind you and hug you like that.'
'Why?'
'So I can stroke your breasts at the same time.'
'OK.'
I climbed behind her and wrapped my skeletal legs around her torso, until my hard on was pressing into her back. I then hugged her tightly and kissed her neck as I did so.
'That was nice,' she informed me.
'Good, I'm glad I was more useful than this morning.'
'I'm glad too. Are you still horny?'
'What do you think?'
'Well something tells me you are.' She reached her hand around and began to stroke me. 'One minute, let me just turn round.'
She knelt up and turned around, I turned my head to look at the ceiling and hide the patch against the back of the tub.
'Lift yourself out of the water,' she ordered putting her hands under my arse and lifting.
I lifted as far as I could.
'You're gonna have to slide your head under the water a bit, so I can get it fully out of the water.'
'Look Rebecca, it really doesn't matter.'
'Slide!' she commanded pulling my arse with such force that my whole body moved lifting my hard on out of the water and forcing my head into it.
'Jesus!'
'Just shh, and enjoy,' she whispered placing me in her mouth.
'Oh my God.'
'You like that?'

'I fucking love it.'

...

'How do you do that thing that women do with the towel on their head?' I asked Rebecca as I climbed out the bath, making sure I faced her the whole time.
'What thing?'
'You know…this thing.' I pulled the towel from the rail and cast it over my head quickly. 'Where you wrap it into like a turban.'
'Come here, I'll do it for you.'
'No just show me and I'll do my own.'
'You do it like this.'
I followed her instructions and wrapped the towel into a tight bunch on my hair.
'What's the point in you doing it? You don't even have long hair.'
'I don't know,' I replied. 'I've always wondered how to. No man can ever perfect that procedure, yet every single woman can. It's kind of like skipping.'
'Whatever you say sweetie. What we gonna do today anyway?'
'I don't know. I have to go back to my place to get a fresh uniform for tonight. Then maybe we could meet up for dinner.'
'I could come to your place with you if you like.'
'Er, not just yet,' I said thinking of the hair loss products scattered round the place. 'It's a bit of a mess, I'd be embarrassed. Maybe you could come round tomorrow though.'
'I'll be working tomorrow morning and you'll be working in the night.'

'Well Wednesday then. That's my rest day this week, would you like to stay at mine Wednesday night?'
'Yes, I'd like that. You can tell a lot about a man by his apartment you know.'
'Really?'
'Really.'

Chapter 18

I arrived at work that evening with a grin on my face. Rebecca and I had just enjoyed dinner and drinks and I was in the mood to put my feet up, maybe catch forty winks when things quietened down. Sundays were still busy, but they were low maintenance, none of the piss heads that we got on Fridays or Saturdays losing their keys or forgetting room numbers. I relieved Janet, watched her pull away out of the car park and set about polishing off a can of Strongbow, while reading the News of the World.

I must have dozed off within half an hour, which is testament to the quality of writing in that particular newspaper, only to be awoken shortly after eleven by the sound of the telephone ringing.

'Good evening Travel Inn, Leeds,' I garbled into the mouthpiece.

'Is that Paul?' hissed a male voice on the other end.

'Er yes, who's this please?'

'Andy.'

'...'

'Hello?'

'Yes, hello. I'm here.'

'How's business mate?' Andy asked.

'Um, not bad, the hotel's full.'

'No, I mean your business.'

'I'm not sure what you're talking about.'

'Oh you know what I'm talking about mate. I'm talking about your little sideline, renting out broken rooms. Was that a prostitute in there the other night? Are you some sort of pimp?'

'No!'

'So what the fuck is going on? I want to know.'

'Nothing's going on and I'm certainly not a pimp.'

'Don't play all innocent with me pal. I know you're up to something and I want in.'

'In on what?'

'I've warned you already fuckwit, don't play innocent. Either you tell me what's going on or I go see Brent first thing tomorrow morning and you lose your job *and* your nice little sideline.'

'There is no sideline.'

'Fine, then I'll see Brent tomorrow and tell him what happened the other night.'

'No, don't do that.'

'Then I want in. Are you selling the rooms by the night or by the hour?'

'Meet me tomorrow morning. I finish at six, what time do you start?'

'Seven thirty.'

'Fine well shall we call it six thirty then? We can meet at the greasy spoon round the corner for breakfast. We'll talk business there.'

'Fine, six thirty for breakfast. You can buy, what with all that extra money you're earning.'

'Fine, see you tomorrow morning.' I snarled, slamming down the phone.

I was too scared to get to sleep again after that. I could feel the adrenaline pumping through my arteries and veins. The first signs of the dreaded panic attacks, that I thought I had beaten, began to manifest themselves. Sweaty palms, thumping heartbeat, tunnel vision and the irresistible urge to just run the fuck away. I drained what was left of the cider to try to calm myself down but it was no good, the adrenaline was fuelling a heart rate that felt like it was in cardiac arrest territory. Time to do a fire check, I thought jumping out of my seat as the fight or flight instinct sent a jolt of electricity down my left arm.

...

I managed to eventually burn off the nervous energy by completing continuous fire and car park checks. I was too panicky to sit still and actually thought about vacuuming reception and cleaning the windows too, but couldn't access the cleaner's cupboard without a key.

Eventually six o' clock came and I was relieved from the desk by Katie another non-descript receptionist. I didn't hang around to chat, I just grabbed my things and left. With half an hour before I met Andy, I thought it prudent to have a bit of a jog, help calm myself down before the showdown.

I jogged for twenty minutes and then made my way to the café round the corner from the hotel. It was open, but empty. I ordered a tea and placed myself in the far corner where I could see the door. It was an obsessive compulsive instinct of mine to prefer a seat where I could see the exit, while in a high stress situation. I watched the door intently for the next ten minutes until eventually a tired looking Andy wondered in and ordered a coffee and a traditional English breakfast from the counter.

'Put it on his tab,' the cunt informed the waitress. She looked over to me for confirmation and I nodded to her to indicate that it was alright. He collected his coffee and swaggered over to my table, a cocky sneer on his face.

'Morning Andy.'

'Morning. Business a bit slow last night then was it?'

'Look Andy, I don't know what you think I'm doing but believe me I am not doing it every night, just Friday and Saturday.'

'Sure you are pal, sure you are. Don't prostitutes work through the week then?'

'Keep your voice down. How do you know Brent isn't a regular in this place?'

'Easy tiger, look around, the place is empty.'

'Yes you stupid fuck, but he might well know the owner or the waitress. Just keep it to a whisper OK?'

'OK,' he whispered. 'But don't try fucking fobbing me off with this weekend only bullshit.'

'Andy, I'm telling you, I only rent the rooms out on Friday and Saturday nights. I am not a pimp, I'm just renting out a couple of rooms to Winston's on their busy nights. They don't need them during the week as they have enough rooms of their own.'

'So how much do you make?'

'Tenner an hour,' I lied.

'I want half.'

'What?'

'You heard me, I want half.'

'And what exactly do I get out of this?'

Well for a start I don't say shit to Brent, that should be your number one concern right now. Secondly I won't all of a sudden start doing overtime, making sure there aren't any broken rooms for you to hire to the brothel. Thirdly, I'm thinking of expansion.'

'Expansion?'

'Yes expansion. As the person in charge of maintenance I am in a position where I can doctor a number of rooms so that they are out of commission for a relatively long period of time. Thus allowing you to rent them out through the week too.'

'I told you already, the brothel doesn't need an overflow midweek.'

'Then we get our own girls.'

'What the fuck? From where?'

'I'll think of something. In the meantime I want half your takings from this weekend. I'll make sure there are four rooms out of commission next week so we can maximise our earnings. That way you won't be losing out either eh? Everyone's a winner.'

'Everyone except the owners of the hotel.'

'Fuck the owners of the hotel.'

Chapter 19

The postman was early that morning. He usually delivered at about nine o' clock but he had already been and gone by the time I arrived home at eight fifteen. I picked the package up from the mailbox and looked at the front, it was covered in Indian stamps.

Aha, the Propecia.

Normally I would have gone straight to bed, but I was eager to get started on my next round of treatment so I pulled the tablets out of the packaging and began to read the leaflet that accompanied them, skipping straight to the side effects:

In clinical studies for PROPECIA, a small number of men experienced certain sexual side effects, such as less desire for sex, difficulty in achieving an erection, or a decrease in the amount of semen. Each of these side effects occurred in less than 2% of men and went away in men who stopped taking PROPECIA because of them.

There was no mention of the man tits or acne that some people on Hairlosstalk had complained about, so I wasn't entirely convinced that all potential side effects had been listed. There was a large section explaining that nine out of ten users had experienced improved or maintained hair on the drug. The odds seemed good, I had a ninety percent chance of re-growing my hair and a two percent chance of turning into a spotty faced woman. Frankly those were good enough for me. I downed a tablet, washed it down with a can of cider and settled down to sleep.

...

When I awoke I noted the erection that was pressing into my boxers and thanked God that the equipment was still working, for now. I fired up the computer and began to pour my hopes and aspirations for the wonder drug onto a post on the Hairlosstalk forum. Within an hour there were three replies, all encouraging. You are doing the right thing man, seemed to be the general consensus. But one of the posts made my blood freeze as I read it:

Go for it mate and don't be put off by the dreaded shedding. A few years back I was on Propecia and literally got worse for eight months straight. The shedding started about month three and didn't stop till about month nine by which time I'd lost about fifty percent of my hair. On month ten, my head did a complete 180! I was growing more and it was coming out thicker. It was really weird how fast it turned around. You have to stick it out at least a year. I was living proof. I started back again and now on month six. I'm Shedding pretty bad right now too. My hair got better in first four months and just got worse during the past one. You have to go through these waves until you hit the ten month mark. Whatever you do, DON'T Stop taking Propecia!

What the fuck was shedding? Why didn't it say anything about that shit on the instructions? Surely losing fifty percent of your hair should be referred to as a side effect. Christ on a bike, this stuff sounded like chemotherapy. I typed shedding into the website's search box and hundreds of threads came up. There was even a special discussion forum on the topic of shedding. I skim read a few posts and my hands dripped with sweat as I did so. Apparently shedding was the most common side effect associated with both Propecia *and* Minoxidil. I had been on the Minox for three months now and apparently could expect a good old shed in the next month or so. The computer's keyboard was soaking now. Jesus, it was from my hands, they were dripping with sweat. I logged off and did fifty sit ups to ward away the impending panic attack from reading the posts.

'Forty eight...forty nine...fifty,' I counted as I completed the last sit up.

Fifty sit ups.

Fifty.

Fifty percent of his hair.

Fifty percent! I tried to imaging my appearance minus fifty percent of my hair. The sweat faucets opened up again, accompanied by the tunnel vision. Press ups, I panicked, try press ups.

'One...two...three.'

...

I eventually managed to calm down by deluding myself that the Toppik would help cover the worst of the shedding. If it didn't I would just have to resort to Permacap. But what about Rebecca? That was the real problem. This was the first relationship I'd had for a while and now I faced losing her as well as a large percentage of the hairs that were currently covering my pate. Why hadn't she come along twelve months from now, when the shedding had passed?

There was no way I could tell her. Not after she had used the words mutilating and baldness in the same sentence. I would rather just end it now. The problem was, I really liked the girl.

Could this relationship be any more complicated?

Chapter 20

Two days later things *did* become more complicated when I discovered on Wednesday afternoon, to my horror, that I was unable to properly maintain an erection.

My suspicions were first aroused when I woke at two in the afternoon to discover that, for the first time in my living memory, a fully tumescent appendage was not digging into my boxer shorts. Concerned by this suspicious turn of events I fired up my PC and clicked on the *Erection Section* icon on my desktop where I kept my pornography. After almost an hour of struggling with my marshmallow like dick I gave up on the computer and began to pace the apartment chewing my nails.

Was this was temporary? Or Psychological? Perhaps it was nothing to do with the Propecia. It might even be the Erection Section, after all I had seen that stuff a hundred times. Maybe I needed some new porn or even better the real thing, I would be seeing Rebecca again that night. Maybe things would be different with her. But what if it wasn't? What if I couldn't manage to get an erection for Rebecca? It was a pretty physical relationship, I couldn't imagine her being impressed by my lack of wood. Think man, think.

Winston's.

I had been meaning to pop over there anyway, to inform Monique that there would be four rooms available at the hotel that weekend instead of the usual two. Maybe I should ask Monique for a freebie to celebrate the good news and request Mai Lee. If that horny little bitch couldn't get me hard, it might be time for a trip to the doctors, get myself a prescription for some Viagra.

Winston's it was.

...

When I arrived, the place was quiet. Just five girls and one punter all playing pool in bathrobes. The guy was probably in his forties, but with a grey beard that made him look older. He seemed dismayed to see another man in the place, no doubt miffed that he would no longer have the undivided attention of the harem. Mai Lee was working and smiled when she recognised me.

'Hiii, you looky for Monique?'

'Yes Mai Lee, is she in?'

'Yes, I go find.'

'Thanks.'

I ogled her sweet, sweet butt as she wiggled it to the back office, then shuddered as Monique's fat arse appeared a minute later.

Beauty and the fucking beast.

'What can I do for you?'

'I've come to tell you that as of this weekend there will be four rooms available to your girls instead of the usual two.'

'How come?'

'I've been rumbled by the maintenance man, but he's willing to keep quiet as long as I cut him in. In fact he's going to make sure that four rooms are permanently out of operation.'

'Well that is good news to me.'

'I thought so.'

'So why didn't you just call and tell me? Why the impromptu visit?'

'Well I was kind of hoping you might let me have a bit of fun with one of the girls, to celebrate the good news.'

'Why wouldn't I? This is a brothel not a fucking convent.'

'No I mean, er, on the house.'

'Oh, on the house eh? And do you intend to let me use the extra rooms at the hotel on the house?'

'Well I...'

'No you don't, do you? Let me get one thing straight pal. This thing we have got running in your hotel is a business agreement, not a friendship. What's more, those girls out there, they are not slaves. I don't fucking own them, they are merely another form of business partner. See that girl over there, that's Mai Lee PLC and she's chairman of the fucking board. How do you think Mai Lee PLC would react if I started telling her to hand out freebies? She'd see that as some sort of hostile takeover and would be looking to consolidate her accounts with a different brothel. You understand?'

'Yes I understand.'

'Right, now we have got that sorted out, I will, just this once, wave my cut of the takings for this particular transaction. Pick a girl and pay her directly. She'll let you know how much.'

'Thanks.'

'Don't mention it, and don't ever come asking for a discount again.'

'I won't,' I replied casting my eye over the five girls round the pool table. They were all attractive in some way or another but Mai Lee was head and shoulders above the rest of them.

'Is Mai Lee available?'

'Why don't you ask her?' Monique spat, turning her back on me and heading back to the office.

'I will,' I said to her back before turning again to the girls. 'Mai Lee?'

'Yes?'

'Can I have a word?'

'Yes.'

'Hi I have just spoken to Monique about you and she says that I should ask you how, er...'

'Fifty pound,' she interrupted, all businesslike.

'Fifty pounds, I think I can manage that.' I began to dig around in my wallet. There was about seventy in there, enough for a nice tip if she was as good as I hoped. 'Yes, that sounds fine.'

I handed her the fifty and she whipped it into her purse.

'Come,' she said grabbing my hand and leading me into one of the rooms.

'Mai Lee?' I whispered as she pushed me onto the bed and began removing my jeans.

'Yes?'

'Can we start with a massage?' I had heard that Thai women gave especially sensuous massages.

'Yes, I give you special massage. Extra twenty pound,' the money grabbing bitch replied, no doubt having spotted the extra cash in my wallet.

'Never mind, I'll just make do with the fuck thanks.' I lay back and gazed at the mirrored ceiling. Her clothes were off and I watched her olive skinned back writhing around as she attempted to massage some life into my cock.

'Hmmm,' she groaned disingenuously, as though playing with my putty like penis was somehow stimulating to her. 'Nice dick, nice and big.'

No it wasn't I thought, it had never been particularly large and it certainly wasn't at the moment.

'Yes so good. Me like.'

What? What was good? What did she like? Jesus this woman's phoniness was doing less for me than the Erection Section. Even the semi on was starting to wane now.

'Yeah, come on big dick, come on.'

'Mai Lee?'
'You want massage now?'
'No I just want to stop.'
'You no like me?'
'Yes, I like. It's just I think I like someone else more.'
'Me still keep money!' she demanded, sitting up.
'Yes you still keep money.'
I pulled my jeans back on and lay back on the bed.
'Do you mind if we stay in here for a while?' I asked her.
'Why?'
'I don't want the girls to think I came quickly.'
'What you want to do?'
'Just talk. Or you could give me that massage, as you're not going to fuck me.'
'Extra twenty quid.'
'What, even though I'm not getting a shag?'
'Me use special massage oil. Vely expensive.'
'Make it ten pounds.'
'Okay, give you special, ten pound back massage,' she stated turning me over onto my front.

I buried my head into the pillow, closed my eyes and sobbed quietly as she expertly massaged my back. My relationship with Rebecca was doomed. Bony, bald and impotent, what sort of catch was that?

Chapter 21

I cancelled my date with Rebecca that night, on the pretext of being ill. She didn't grill me too hard, she just asked what was wrong with me. The shits, I informed her, the Tijuana Cha Cha. My next call was to the doctors to make an appointment for the following morning. The twat could squeeze me in at nine thirty I was informed.

After hanging up the phone I logged onto Hairlosstalk and began a new chapter on my hair loss blog detailing the latest cruel twist of events in the conflict with my disfigurement. I then spent twenty minutes taking digital photographs of the state of my hairline and saving them on the computer, complete with dates, so that I would have a good idea how my hairline progressed/regressed as my treatment continued. The photographs made depressing viewing, especially as I took them under a harsh light to highlight the full extent of the follicular carnage.

When my hair had dried, I inspected the rear of my head again, using the aligned mirrors and to my great surprise I noticed that there were in fact new hairs growing at the back. Oh my God, I almost screamed, before inspecting again, more thoroughly. Jesus, there really were new hairs coming through. Not dark ones, but thin bum fluffy whiskers emanating from my tonsure. That must be the Minoxidil. The shit was actually beginning to work, thank God. And this was just the beginning, once the Propecia kicked in I should be able to thicken these vellous hairs up a little.

The re-growth rollercoaster ride was on the up again.

Chapter 22

My GP, Doctor Collins, looked less than impressed to see me in his office again.

'What can I do for you this time Mr Hisky?'

'Well it's about my hair loss.'

'I thought we discussed this already. I gave you a couple of options for your hair loss remember. Minoxidil or Propecia if I remember correctly.'

'Yes, yes you did, and I am currently taking both medications.'

'So what exactly do you require from me now?'

'Viagra.'

'Viagra is not a treatment for baldness Mr Hisky, it is a treatment used for people suffering from impotence.'

'I know that.'

'And are you suffering from impotence?'

'Of course I am you imbecile. Why else would I be here humiliating myself in front of you?'

Doctor Collins stared at me for a long moment over the rim of his spectacles, I thought for a moment he was actually going to challenge me to a fight.

'Mr Hisky, I do not appreciate being abused by you or anyone else in my own surgery. If you are not careful I shall have you ejected from the building and may even force you to find yourself another GP.'

'Sorry, it's just a sensitive subject. I find all this very embarrassing.'

'I'm sure you do. When did the impotence start?'

'Yesterday.'

'Yesterday?'

'Yes, yesterday.'

'Mr Hisky, I hardly think that the inability to achieve an erection on one occasion constitutes impotence.'

'Trust me Doctor, if you had seen the girl you would know that this *must* be impotence.'

'No, I mean that one occasion doesn't represent a serious enough problem for me to start prescribing drugs. You may have simply been stressed, or drunk.' He said the last part with a heavy emphasis on drunk.

'I was not drunk. I believe that the impotence is caused by the Propecia I am taking for my hair loss. One of the potential side effects is impotence.'

'Then stop taking Propecia.'

'Not an option I'm afraid.'

'Well until you stop taking Propecia I do not intend to start prescribing medicines to a man with a history of prescription drug dependence.'

'That was a long time ago and I hardly think Viagra is in the same league as tranquillisers.'

'Nevertheless I will not entertain the idea of prescribing Viagra until you have been off the Propecia for two weeks and only then will I prescribe it if the impotence persists for a prolonged period of time.'

'Thanks Doc, thanks a lot.'

'Anytime,' the four eyed bastard smirked.

I was not without a back up plan. There were people who I could obtain Viagra from without a prescription; it's just that it would cost a hefty sum of money compared to a doctor's prescription.

I procured twenty tablets that same afternoon from a bar in town called Big Lil's which was known for fencing stolen goods and selling illegal and prescription drugs. The huge beast of a man that sold me them demanded five pounds per pill which was ten times what I would have paid on the NHS and they were not even proper Viagra tablets. They were called Ramagra or something. But still, he assured me that a couple of hours after taking one of these bad boys I would be so horny I would even be willing to shag the two tonne oil mountain that was serving behind the bar. No way, I mused as I eyed the portly lass.

Chapter 23

Three hours, six pints and two Ramagra tablets later I was starting to see the old boiler behind the bar in a different light. She wasn't quite as rotund as I had originally thought. She still wasn't particularly attractive but there was something about her. I sat and watched the horny bitch as she collected the empty glasses from the table next to mine and caught a sneak peak at her mammoth mammary glands while she wiped the table. As she stood up and turned around I eyeballed her ass and pondered whether I might be able to talk her into giving me a quick nosh in the bogs. As she moved away towards the bar I looked across the room to Jack, the bearded warrior that had sold me the Ramagra and he nodded at me knowingly before motioning his eyes towards the barmaid. Jesus, what was I doing ogling this bitch? The tablets were obviously working, why the hell didn't I just go round to Rebecca's and work off the Ramagra on her? Yes that's what I'd do, give Rebecca a call and ask her if it was all right to pop around.
 'Hello?' Rebecca answered after a prolonged ringing.
 'Hi Rebecca, it's me. Can I come around?'
 'Where are you? You sound drunk.'
 'I'm just in Big Lil's.'
 'Haven't you got to work tonight?'
 'Not until Ten.'
 'Paul, it's seven o' clock now. There's no way you are going to sober up in time for work.'
 'I'll be fine.'
 'No you won't. Anyway I thought you were ill, what the hell are you doing out drinking if you're not well?'
 Shit, I forgot I had cancelled our date the night before.
 'I'm better now.'

'Well you better phone the hotel and tell them that you are sick. If you go in like that you are liable to get the sack.'

'Can I come round your place if I phone in sick?'

'No.'

'Why not? I really want to see you.'

'You should have come round last night if you wanted to see me so badly.'

'So it's like that is it?'

'Like what?'

'You're mad at me for being ill yesterday.'

'No you dickhead, I am mad at you for being pissed when you have work in three hours. It's a little immature you know.'

'OK sorry, I'll phone in sick then shall I?'

'Yes I think you should.'

'Am I slurring?'

'Yes.'

'Badly?'

'Very.'

'Will you call in for me? If I call they will know I'm pissed. I might lose my job.'

'And who the hell am I supposed to say I am? Your mother or something?'

'Yes, tell them you are my mother. Tell them I am too sick to call in myself.'

'I'll do it, but believe me I am not happy about this. Not happy at all. Now give me the number.'

I was definitely in the cunt book here. I gave her the number and she hung up, without even saying goodbye.

Still, at least I had the night off work.

...

I didn't go back in Big Lil's but chose instead to scour the streets and bars of Leeds for something mildly attractive to fuck. Whether it was the stench of desperation, the drunkenness or just my plain old ugliness I'll never know. But what I do know is this, no one in Leeds seemed to want to fuck me and I had never been so horny in my life.

I even considered going into a gay bar.

After a couple more hours of rejection and drink I ingested a third Ramagra and withdrew a hundred quid from my hair implants account then made my merry way down to Winston's.

The outside of the building looked different at night, more dingy. There was uncollected garbage and discarded food strewn along the pavement outside and a couple of rats scurried away from the door as I approached it. From one of the windows I could hear the creaking wood of the bed and the groaning of the room's occupants which along with the vile stench of the garbage and the vermin gave me the strange impression of being outside the hull of the Amistad.

'Evening Monique,' I greeted the madame as I entered.

'Evening Paul. To what do I owe the pleasure?'

'Nothing, I have not come to see you I have merely come to indulge in the carnal arts.'

'I hope you're not expecting another discount?'

'Of course not. Is Mai Lee working?'

'Yes but she is already occupied at the moment.'

'I'll wait.'

'There's plenty of other girls in here.'

'I'll wait.'

It had to be Mai Lee, the humiliation of yesterday's experience was still raw. I had to show her I was a real man. Prove to her that yesterday had been a one off. I ordered a drink from the bikini clad bartender and sat watching two of the girls fussing over a punter in a towel. They were each trying to convince him to take a sauna with them and eventually he ended up taking both. They giggled as they each took him by a hand and led him towards the sauna room.

Eventually Mai Lee emerged from a room with a man who looked like he was old enough to be my grandfather. He was easily seventy odd years old, silver haired, flat cap and a walking stick! Unbelievably there was not a trace of embarrassment on the coffin dodging bastard's wrinkly old face, instead he was smiling like he had just won a tenner at the bingo. Christ, here I was about to stir this old fucker's porridge and *I* was the one that needed Ramagra. Still it comforted me a little to think that just because you were in your seventies you needn't be out of the game. This noble gentleman was living proof of that. Mai Lee gave him a kiss on the cheek and he handed her a couple of notes which I assumed to be a tip. She kissed him again and patted his bottom while leading him to the exit.

When he had gone she counted the money he had handed her, which looked to me to be about thirty quid. She smiled and put it in her handbag.

'Mai Lee,' I called her over.
'Hello. You come back see me again?'
'Yes I come back see you again.'
'Want massage?'
'Er, no. I want the other thing.'
'OK, no more discount. Eighty pound. You pay Monique.'

I paid Monique and let Mai Lee lead me into the room. It was a different one from yesterday, no mirrors on the roof, but plenty around the rest of the room.

'You take clothes off,' Mai Lee commanded as she whipped off her dress, leaving her heels on.

I stumbled around drunkenly as I attempted to remove my shoes and socks. Mai watched me, no doubt expecting me to be easy money again after yesterday's performance. When my socks were off I lay back on the bed and asked her to remove my jeans for me.

'OK,' she agreed, strutting over to me in her heels.

I closed my eyes as she began to unbutton me slowly while massaging my groin through the denim.

'You vely hard this time,' she noted.

'Yes very hard. Very pleased to see you that's why.'

'You vely, vely please to see me.'

She pulled my shorts over the massive erection I was now sporting and I opened my eyes as she did so. Fuck me, this stuff was like an instant penis enlarger. I had never seen myself looking so large. Mai Lee straddled me and began to stroke my testicles softly.

'You want me give you sucky?'

'Yes I want.'

'OK,' she said lowering her breasts onto my face. I kissed them and she made a fake groan. I didn't care this time I just wanted to drill the shit out of her.

The breasts moved further south, rubbing against my chest, then my stomach and finally my groin. She pushed her breasts together, clamping my concrete dick in them, before sliding it into her mouth at the same time.

'Ohhh, fuck,' I moaned.

'You like?'

'I fucking love.'

Outside I could hear something of a commotion, but I didn't give a shit. It was no doubt some pissed up punter demanding a refund for a shit fuck. I on the other hand knew I was about to have the ride of a lifetime. I had chosen wisely, God bless Mai Lee.

'What that?' Mai Lee asked removing me from her mouth.

'Nothing,' I replied, pushing her back onto it.

'I hear something.'

'It's outside. It doesn't matter. Please Mai Lee, I am bursting here.'

She placed me back in her mouth and began revolving her well practised tongue around the glans. The noise outside grew louder as I neared climax. Mai Lee was well tuned into my excitement and began to quicken her pace involving her hands in the blowjob as she did so. Faster and faster the strokes became as I grew more and more animated. Any minute now and I would be spraying myself all over her, I thought in delight.

'Open up,' came a voice from outside the door accompanied by a heavy knock on the door. 'West Yorkshire Police, this is a raid.'

Chapter 24

I awoke, with a raging hangover and an erection I could have hung my coat from, in what appeared to be a police cell. I groaned and rubbed my eyes. My belt had been removed and so had my top. There was very little inside the cell except for the concrete bed and wafer thin mattress that I was lying upon. I lifted myself up and staggered towards the door.

'Hello!' I shouted as I banged upon the heavy door.

No Answer.

'Hello! I'm awake now, can you process me please?'

Still no answer. I banged again and shouted but a reply never came so I gingerly placed myself back on the concrete bed. Despite my predicament and hangover I was still as horny as I had been while in the clutches of Mai Lee. If they would only process me quickly I could go home and abuse myself in front of the computer.

I glanced again at the door, no one was coming, that much was evident. I didn't even know what time it was due to the artificial light in the cell. For all I knew I might have only been in there for an hour or two. After all, judging by the ferocity of my erection, the Ramagra was still going strong.

This was typical of the joke that was my life; cured of my impotence I was about to have the most explosive orgasm of my life and had instead ended up getting myself arrested. Unbelievable. If only they had arrived a couple of minutes later. I closed my eyes and imagined what it would have been like exploding all over Mai Lee. Good God that woman had a talented mouth.

What was taking so long?

I eventually resigned myself to the fact that I wouldn't be getting released anytime soon and tried to get back to sleep. No joy, I was too hung-over and horny to sleep. I couldn't get tits and arses out of my head. My mind remorselessly replayed images of Mai Lee's head bobbing up and down on my penis. You vely hard...You vely hard...You vely hard.

I was very hard, very hard indeed. Sleep was not an option. I looked at the door. Where were they? What was taking so long?

Fuck it.

I turned myself over so my back was facing the door and slid my shorts over the solid slab within them. Spitting onto my palm for lubrication I began to massage the glans of my penis, slowly at first then faster. You vely hard. Yes me very fucking hard now suck harder you dirty bitch...yeh that's it c'mon...yeh.

I didn't give a fuck now whether the police walked in on me or not, I just wanted the relief. I flipped onto my back and pulled the sheets below my waist so I could stare at the majestic hard on I was sporting. Fuck me if I'd had a camera I would've taken a picture, it was that impressive. With the mixture of saliva and pre-come my bell end was shining like a generalissimo's jack boots, and I could see a miniature reflection of my face on it. I toyed with the idea of trying to give myself a blowjob but reasoned I was still a good foot short. Instead I revived the image of Mai Lee's sensational blowjob as I screwed my face in anticipation of reaching climax.

'Oh Christ,' I screamed as I coughed the filthy yogurt all over my stomach. 'Fuck me.'

With the relief of the orgasm came the realisation that I was, at present, in a police cell with a subsiding hard on in my hand and half a gallon of spunk on my stomach and chest. What the hell was I thinking? I quickly whipped off my socks and utilised them as a Wankerchief in a hasty mopping up before turning them inside out and putting them back on my feet. The soggy warmth of the spunk felt wet and uncomfortable on my feet and I once again found myself wishing that the police would just hurry up and get me processed.

...

'Mr Hisky,' a voice eventually announced as the heavy iron door of the cell opened.
'Yes, that's me.'
'Can you put your shoes back on and come with me please?' he said, throwing me the laces to my shoes.
'Yes, are you letting me go now?'
'Soon Mr Hisky, first of all we need to charge you.'
'Charge me? What with?'
'Sex with a prostitute and battery.'
'Battery, what the hell is that?'
'Touching someone without their permission.'
'What do you mean without their permission? She was a prostitute for God's sake. I got her permission when I paid my eighty quid.'
'I am not talking about the girl you were found in the room with Mr Hisky, I am referring to your arresting officer.'
'What you mean I tried to fondle a female police officer?'
'The arresting officer was actually a man.'
'...'
'A big hairy man.'
'...'
'Put your shoes on please.'
I put my shoes on and desperately tried to recall the moment of my arrest but could not remember anything after the door had been opened and the two officers

entered. Christ, they *were* both men and one of them *was* big and hairy.

'Am I looking at jail?'

'That would depend on whether PC Thompson wants to press charges.'

'Oh dear God.'

The detention officer led me from my cell into an interview room, where I was fingerprinted and a swab taken for my DNA. Eventually another officer came in and sat at the opposite end of the desk from me.

'Now then Mr Hisky we'll get you processed shall we?'

'Err, yes. I am so sorry about this; it's not like me at all. I have never been arrested before, I think someone must have spiked my drink. I couldn't help myself, I was so horny. It's the first time I have ever visited a brothel and I've certainly never fondled a ma...'

'Please Mr Hisky, before you carry on, we do check prisoner's possessions when we book them in you know and we did find several Ramagra tablets on your person at the time.'

'OK so I did procure the Ramagra myself, but that's not illegal is it? I admit I shouldn't have visited the brothel but it was the first time ever. As for touching the police officer, I am so sorry. Could you apologise to him for me?'

'Have you been winding him up Terry?' the constable said, turning to the detention officer.

'Yes,' he replied laughing, then turned to me. 'Sorry mate, I couldn't resist it.'

'You mean I didn't fondle a man?'

'No, but you did *think* you had, which is pretty worrying.'

They were both laughing now. I felt a wave of indignity surge inside me. These bastards had ignored my calls in the cell for hours and now they were trying to make me think I had turned gay.

'You bastard,' I snapped. 'You leave me in that cell for hours shouting for you to let me out and you pull a dirty trick like that. Real professional! Real, fucking, professional mate. No wonder people can't stand the police.'

'Sorry mate.'

'Sorry? I screamed indignantly. 'Sorry? I could've been hanging myself in that cell. What if, I'd have strung myself up after you had fucking ignored my calls? That would've been funny wouldn't it? Walking in on a corpse?'

'Not possible.'

'Of course it's possible. You think because I didn't have a belt or shoe laces I couldn't have hung myself? I could've used my jeans couldn't I? Did you think about that? No! So I suggest the next time you ignore someone when they are shouting in their cell, you tear yourself away from your TV or Playstation, or whatever it is you fucking do that's so important and you answer the fucking calls, dickhead! In fact I am seriously thinking of making a complaint, what are your names?'

'No I mean it's not possible because we have CCTV cameras in every cell. You are being constantly monitored and I would have known if you were preparing to hang yourself.'

'...'

'Do you understand Mr Hisky? You needn't have been concerned for your own safety as I was watching you from the moment you woke up.'

'...'

'Shall we get on with processing you?' the constable interjected, with a smirk on his face.

'Yes let's just do that,' I replied.

'Do you still want our names?' the detention officer sniggered.

Chapter 25

I got home at about ten in the morning and after showering I pulled myself around the room for another hour or two. I just couldn't help it. That Ramagra was some real potent shit.

I placed the tablets in the medicine cabinet, showered again and began to apply a liberal quantity of Minoxidil. I was paranoid now that I had missed last night's application, spent the night in jail *and* missed a Propecia tablet. Not a good start to my day at all really.

When my hair dried I aligned the mirrors to check on the general state of the patch. It looked pretty good upon close inspection, some of the vellous hairs were starting to darken, in almost exactly the same way my first pubes had done when I was thirteen years old. But when viewed with the mirror held further away and under the light, these hairs could hardly be seen at all. I thanked God once more for the invention of Toppik and began to shake a generous quantity over the patch, within seconds it was starting to fill in.

I had just covered the perimeter of the circle closest to my forehead when I realised that the flow of particles was noticeably restricted. What the fuck? I held the can in front of my face and shook it onto the palm of my hand. A smattering of tiny grains rained from the can but nothing like the amount I was used to. I weighed the can in my hand, it didn't feel particularly empty. Strange. I then took a corkscrew from the sink and stuck it into each of the can's sprinkling holes to make sure they were not blocked, then shook it above my palm once again.

Hardly anything. Shit.

That meant the can was virtually empty. Those bastards had made it so heavy you could hardly tell when it was almost finished. What the hell was I going to do now? I fired up the PC and immediately ordered a year's supply of Toppik and an industrial amount of Minoxidil and Propecia while I was at it. It cost me the best part of three hundred pounds but I wasn't about to fall prey to this shit again.

I ordered the Toppik from a supplier in the UK who claimed they would dispatch within two days. It cost me an extra fifty quid altogether but I would have probably paid my last six months savings to procure it. I felt like a junkie, desperate for my next fix and realised with desperation that I was a slave to all three products now. No doubt I would have sold my house and all its contents to fuel this dreadful habit. Where would this end? Would I find myself prostituting myself to other men in a couple of year's time, just to feed my addictions?

I prised the top off the can of Toppik with a pen knife and scraped out the remains of the fibres onto my palm, then rubbed it into the area of my scalp that was still exposed.

It appeared to veil the patch when the harsh white lamp in the bathroom was switched off, but when I switched the lamp on again the shiny white flesh was all too easy to distinguish and having been suppressed for so long under the cloak of Toppik it looked worse than ever, like I had gone bald overnight.

…

I really didn't want to go to work that night, but I needed the money. My savings had been hit hard by the bulk purchases that I had made during the afternoon and I couldn't afford to lose a day's pay. I waved Janet off from the premises at ten on the dot and began setting about a couple of cans of cider.

When she had gone I pulled out my old vanity mirror and a new one I had purchased that afternoon. The difference that I had seen in the patch earlier with and without the bathroom light on had made me conscious of the effect that luminosity had upon the general appearance of my tonsure.

Light was the enemy.

I aligned the mirrors and satisfied myself that the patch was indeed difficult to spot in this particular room; which was probably due to the fact that the ceilings were high in here, unlike my bathroom where the lamp was just above my head.

This was an exact science. The brightness and proximity were obviously equally important factors.

Two hours into the shift I was fast asleep in the back office when the bell rang on the reception desk. Fuck me, some pissed up old bastard had no doubt lost his key or forgotten his room number, I thought.

I groaned and rubbed my eyes, before peering through the peephole to make sure the place wasn't being held up. It wasn't. It was that twat Andy, the maintenance guy, waiting patiently at the customer side of the counter. What the fuck did he want? Did he expect another free room for him and his girlfriend again?

'Hello Andy,' I snapped as I stumbled out into the reception hall.

'Now then mate, how's business?'

'We're full. Are you wanting a room for you and your lass again or something?'

'No, I just came to talk business with you.'

'Yeah, well I'm not even sure there is gonna be a business anymore,' I said, thinking of the raid that the police had made on Winston's last night.

'What? Of course there is. Business is going to boom now you've got me as a partner.'

'I wouldn't count on that old bean. There's no guarantee that Winston's is going to open again, and I mean ever again. There was a police raid over there last night.'

'Yes I know.'

'Oh, I didn't realise it was in the local papers.'

'I'm not sure it was.'

'So how did you hear about it?'

'I saw it.'

'Wow, really? Where were you?'

'Over here.'

'What? Fixing a room at that time of night?'

'No, I was here to watch the raid.'

'Eh?'

'I told you we were going to expand mate, well now we can use the rooms seven days a week.'

'What?'

'Now that the police have closed Winston's down we can run a full time operation. I'll make sure that there are about six or seven rooms permanently out of operation and we can start to renegotiate our arrangement with the owner of the ex-brothel. I think you'll agree that we are now in a much stronger bargaining position.'

'How the hell did you know about the raid?'

'How do you think?'

'Enlighten me.'

'I tipped the police off.'

'You did what?' I screamed moving towards him with my fists clenched.

'I tipped them off. I had to be clever about it though. The fuckers weren't particularly interested in a massage parlour. Not until I told them that they were using illegal immigrants that is. Sex slaves, I called them. Pretty crafty eh?'

'I'll give you crafty you fuckwit,' I yelled, lunging at the fucking moron.

'Woah,' Andy said, ducking away from my wild swing. 'What the fuck is wrong with you? I just increased our potential earnings by about three hundred percent.'

'You just got me fucking arrested, that's what you did,' I replied, advancing on him again.

'What the hell are you talking about?'

'I'm talking about the fact that I was in the fucking brothel when the police made the raid, dickhead. Why the hell didn't you tell me what you were planning to do?'

Andy held his palms out in submissively, backing away from me as he did so. He looked scared, and so he should, I was fully intent upon kicking his fucking arse.

'Calm down mate, how was I to know you were in there?'

'If you'd told me what you were planning to do I fucking well wouldn't have been.'

'Look Paul, back off. I know karate so you better not start anything or you'll regret it. Let's just talk about this. Believe me, this is a good thing in the long run. We'll be laughing about this in a couple of weeks.'

Karate my arse. This bastard looked scared, real scared and it didn't matter how many excuses he threw my way. I was going to kick the living shit out of him.

…

'What the hell happened to you?' Rebecca asked staring at the gash above my left eye.

'I got jumped, at the hotel.'

'Jesus! Who jumped you?'

'I don't know, there were about six of them. I disturbed them while they were breaking into a car.'

'My God, have you been to the hospital?'

'No.'

'You should, your eye looks terrible *and* your mouth for that matter. They really went to town on you, those bastards. Six against one! I hope you called the police.'

'Er, no. I just called Brent and told him I quit.'

'Why?'

'I've had enough of that place. I have almost had my arse kicked on a number of occasions and this has just made me realise that it was only a matter of time.'

'Oh you poor thing. Come here,' she said, grabbing me and giving me a tight hug.

'Owww.'

'What?'

'My ribs, I think they're bruised.'

'Those fuckers. We should call the police.'

'No! Er, no, just leave it. I'll be fine in a couple of days, there's no need to involve the police.'

'Of course there is, you can't let them get away with this.'

'Rebecca, I didn't get a decent description of any of them. What the hell are the police gonna do?'

'You didn't get a description of *any* of them?'

'No.'

'Why not?'

'Well I was too busy trying to protect my face and testicles actually. Jesus, I've just had the shit kicked out of me and you're giving me the third degree. I knew I shouldn't have come here.'

'Sorry sweetie,' she replied stroking my arm. 'I was just concerned about you that's all. If you don't want to call the police then we won't but I do think you should go to hospital.'

'No, I'd rather just lie down and relax,' I objected, thinking to myself how ironic it was that I had spent a significant proportion of my life in hospitals and the doctor's surgery for phantom illnesses yet the minute I actually needed a hospital I was refusing to go.

'OK I'll run the bath so you can soak your cuts and bruises.'

'Thanks Rebecca.'

...

'Why are you bathing in the dark?' Rebecca asked as she entered the bathroom to check on me.

' Leave it off please, it's more relaxing. Plus my eye is aching in the light,' I bullshitted her so she didn't switch it on and illuminate the scarcely covered circle of shame.

'Fair enough. Are you going to be much longer?'

'No, why?'

'I was going to give you a nice long massage and maybe even a blowjob if you feel up to it'

'I'll be two minutes.'

I waited until she closed the door, grabbed my jeans from the side of the bath and rummaged frantically for one of the Ramagra pills. Found one. Excellent. I threw it down my neck and stuck my mouth under the bath tap to wash it down.

'Agghhrr!!!'

It was the wrong fucking tap, the hot one. I spat the boiling liquid out and the Ramagra pill flew out too, disappearing into the soapsuds. Why God? Why must I be fucking cursed?

'Paul? Are you alright?' Rebecca asked re-entering the bathroom.

'I think so.'

'Did I hear you screaming?'

'Yes I was washing the cut on my eye and the hot water stung it, that's all.'

'Can I get you anything?'

'Yes, can you get me a glass of water please?'

'Of course, I'll get it now.'

'Rebecca?'

'Yes?'

'Can you put some ice in it please?'

'Of course I can sweetie.'

'Thanks,' I replied, watching the door close and then fishing the Ramagra back out of the tub.

Chapter 26

I awoke to the sound of Rebecca's screaming alarm clock the following morning in a good deal of pain. Funny how a good kicking only really hurts after you've been to sleep. On top of that the humiliation of the pasting I had taken at Andy's hands was beginning to kick in as well. He had given me at least three chances to back off yet I stupidly ignored them all. The one about karate should have made me think twice. What the hell had I been trying to do? I'd not won a fight since high school, and even back then I had lost the majority of them.

'Morning,' Rebecca said, rubbing her eyes and then giving me a kiss on the cheek. 'Are you feeling better today?'

'Not really, I'm aching quite a lot.'

'Do you want to stay in bed? I'll leave you the spare key if you like or you could just stay here until I get home.'

'No, I'll leave with you.'

'OK, let me just get a quick shower and we'll get off.'

'OK.'

She climbed out of bed and I gazed in wonder at her body as she walked naked across the bedroom. Fuck me I was lucky to have met this girl, I thought, very lucky indeed.

The minute she was out the room I started to dress myself and when I heard the sound of the shower I pulled the mirrors out of my bag and checked my hair. Bad, real bad. One good reason not to stay here all day, I had to avoid her until the fresh batch of Toppik arrived. Hopefully it might be here this morning, but more likely it would be tomorrow.

The shower stopped and I pulled on my trucker cap and trainers.

'Paul?'

'Yes?'

'Could you bring me a towel? There isn't one in here, you left it in the bedroom last night.'

'OK,' I replied picking up the towel from the chair and marching into the bathroom. 'Here you go.'

'Thanks sweetie, aren't you going to have a shower?'

'No, I'm fine. I had my bath last night.'

'How did you enjoy your massage?' she asked rubbing her breasts dry.

'It was amazing, the best ever.'

'Relaxing?'

'Very.'

'It must have been, I tried waking you up with a blowjob but you didn't even get hard.'

'Did you?' I tried to look surprised but could feel my eyes betrayed me. Did she suspect I was pretending to sleep? I hoped not. That fucking Ramagra pill I had fished from the tub had dissolved to about a third of its normal size. If there were any bacteria in that bathwater they would no doubt still be shagging now.

'Yes I did, but you were out for the count.'

'Wow, what a shame. I can't believe I missed out on a blowjob.'

'You missed out on a lot more than that,' she whispered, stroking my groin and kissing my ear.

'Shit, how about tomorrow night?'

'Why not tonight? It's not like you're working or anything.'

'I arranged to meet an old friend tonight.'

'Fair enough,' she snapped, letting go of my genitals and walking out of the bathroom. I wasn't sure whether she was annoyed at me for not being available tonight or the fact that nothing had stirred in my trousers while she groped me.

'Don't be like that Rebecca.'
'Like what?'
'Getting into a huff. I'm sorry but I already arranged to meet my friend. I'll be free tomorrow.'
'I'm not getting into a huff about you meeting your friend, for God's sake. It's you. You run hot and cold. I don't know where I stand with you. I still haven't been to your place yet and you constantly try to duck out of meeting me and then have the cheek to just turn up on my doorstep when you've been beaten up. You're a very strange man do you know that?'
'Of course I fucking know that. My life is fucked, I've got so many inhibitions and neurosis I wouldn't even know where to start. You just have to believe me that I am not ducking out of meeting you because I don't want to see you, It's just that…well…I don't know.'
'What? Tell me for fuck's sake.'
'Just forget about it.'
'See! There you go again, clamming up. Just tell me what's wrong with you.'
'I…I can't.'
'You're married aren't you?'
'No.'
'Then what? What could be so important that you have to act all sneaky and secretive?'
What could I say? Actually I'm not expecting the dyed and shredded sheep's wool, that I have been sprinkling over my hair to conceal my baldness from you, until tomorrow morning? Not likely.
'I've told you forget about it.'
'Fine, I'm gonna be late for work anyway. I don't have time for this shit.'
She dressed in silence and we left for the bus without exchanging a word. I tried to hold her hand at one point

but she spurned it. The weather was shitty, as usual, and we stood quietly waiting at the bus stop.

'Would you like to come round to my place tomorrow?' I asked, trying to break the silence.

'What you expect me to say yes now, just so that you can cancel again tomorrow do you?'

'No, I promise I won't cancel. I'll cook you anything you like and I promise to wake up if you give me a blow job while I'm sleeping.'

'Shut up,' she said, hitting me and looking around to make sure nobody respectable had heard me in the bus shelter. But when she turned back again I noticed she was smiling. Giggling actually. I tentatively reached for her hand and she accepted it this time, even stroking my fingers when she did so.

'I'm sorry,' I whispered.

'So you should be. I can't believe you didn't wake up.'

'Aha so that's what all this was about. I knew it.'

'It wasn't about that, but yes that did piss me off.'

'Like I said, I promise to wake up next time.'

'You better.'

…

The bus was as packed with school kids as usual. Dozens of the screaming mother fuckers hurling missiles around the bus.

'Shit, I hate this fucking bus,' I told her. 'One of us needs to get a car.'

'I need a licence before I can get a car. Why don't you get one? You did, until yesterday, have two incomes after all. What the hell do you do with all that money?'

It's funny you should ask. I'm saving for a hair transplant actually.

'Nothing really I just spend it on clothes and food and stuff.'

'What stuff?'

'You know, stuff.'

'No I don't kno…Jesus! What the fuck?'

'What's wrong?'

'A fucking pen just hit me on the back of the head, that's what's wrong,' she growled getting up and turning around to face the school kids. 'OK which of you little fuckers threw that?'

No response.

I turned around too and tried to look hard, which was pretty difficult when it was painfully obvious I had recently taken a good hiding.

'I said which of you little twats threw that pen?' Rebecca snapped again.

Still no response.

'Well you better fucking calm down back there or I'll have the driver throw you all off.'

The kids just looked at us, some giggled but others looked more menacing. I didn't like this at all, I felt vulnerable with them being behind us and wanted this fucking trip to just end. We turned around again and I asked Rebecca if she was all right.

'Yes,' I heard her reply, after which I just watched her mouth move. I was too busy concentrating on what the school kids were saying behind us. I could hear the word 'bitch' being used a lot and just fucking knew that there was trouble in store. I then watched in dismay as another missile, what looked like an eraser, flew past my head. Then another and another. We were now the targets, sitting ones at that.

'Let's just get off the bus,' I suggested. 'There'll be another one in a minute.'

'No I fucking won't. Will you tell the driver to kick them off please?'

'I'm not sure he can do that.'

'Of course he can, they are being a nuisance. Ask him please.'

I didn't want to let her down again, so despite my reservation I got up and made my way to the front of the bus and had a word with the driver. He was a pretty big bloke with a goatee beard and several tattoos down his Popeye sized forearms. I explained that the school kids were throwing pens and erasers at us and he nodded sympathetically.

'I'll turf them off at the next stop mate,' he growled.

'Thanks.'

He shouldn't have much trouble persuading the little fuckers to disembark, I thought as I retook my seat.

'He's going to throw them off at the next stop,' I told Rebecca as I sat down.

'Thanks,' she replied taking my hand and stroking my fingers. I was definitely back in the good books here.

...

'Right you lot, get off,' the fearsome looking driver barked when we reached the next stop.

They protested for five minutes until it became apparent that the bus would not be setting off again until they alighted. Then, one by one, they began to trudge off. First the more placid of the kids, then the dickheads, the ones that had no doubt been targeting us with the missiles.

'Grassing cunt,' a fifteen year old looking boy hissed at me knocking my head with his schoolbag.

It was obvious that I was the instigator in their expulsion from the bus and they didn't look very happy with me. I made a mental note to stay in bed the next time Rebecca offered me the chance to. All these teenagers sneering and scowling at me brought back haunting memories of some of the dickheads I had been forced to put up with at school.

'Thanks a lot you old bastard,' another snapped as he went past. 'We're gonna have to walk in the rain now.'

'You should've thought about that before you started throwing things around shouldn't you?' I tried my best to look unfazed, but my recent beating and the fact that this evil looking teenager looked a lot like Darren Boyd, my chief tormenter at school had me un-nerved.

Another bag was deliberately hit against my head, then another and I found myself feeling like the school geek rather than a grown man. Then the unthinkable happened, before I could react I felt my cap being pulled from my head and thrown to the front of the bus.

'Give that back,' I shouted in vain as the Darren Boyd look-alike caught it five yards in front of me. I didn't want to get up and chase him because I knew that: He would only throw it again to someone else; Rebecca would surely notice my tonsure; and quite frankly, I was pretty scared of the evil looking bastard.

'Come and get it dickhead.'

'Give it back!' I yelled, trying my best to sound menacing.

'Aaahhh, look!' a voice yelled from behind, 'he's going bald!!!'

Those last words hit me like a sledgehammer, so much so that I scarcely heard anything after that, I just saw the laughing, taunting faces and the fingers pointed towards my hair as about twenty teenagers pissed themselves at my bald patch.'

In a rage I got up and rushed at the Boyd look-alike. Years of buried anger at the treatment Boydie had dished out to me at school manifested itself in that one apoplectic lunge. I watched the teenager's face contort in surprise as I sprang at him, then turn into an evil smile as I got closer and he realised that despite my advantage in years I was probably smaller than he was.

'Give it fucking back!' I yelled above the screams of laughter, fully expecting him to hurl it to another child.

He didn't, he just held onto it while holding me away with his other arm as I used all my pathetic might in a vain attempt to force it from him. The laughter grew louder, and his face more evil as I felt strip after strip of my masculinity being torn painfully away.

I eventually gave up from a combination of exhaustion and the realisation that the whole degrading episode was being recorded by the schoolchildren on their mobile phones.

I looked at Rebecca, who seemed to be in a state of shock, glued to her bus seat. Then turned and fled from the bus.

Chapter 27

Once more unto the bath dear friends, once more. The panic attacks were back with a fucking vengeance. I spent the next week under a self imposed house arrest. Most of the week was spent in an ice cold bath trying to ward away the dreaded heebie jeebies. The rest of it was spent sucking on a cider can in front of the computer scouring sites like You Tube in case any of the Children of the Damned had posted my humiliating experience on there. It appeared that they hadn't. No doubt they were currently Bluetoothing it to one another in the playground though, having a good old laugh at the bald guy trying to retrieve his cap. Oh God, time for another bath.

By the end of the week I had managed to cut down from about thirty full on panic attacks a day to five or six minor ones. I could just about keep them in check with cider alone and eased myself off the cold bath therapy. I still didn't feel like leaving the house though and ordered my groceries and alcohol online from Tesco to prevent myself from starving and sobering up.

I spent the next two days online doing nothing but watching porn and reading the news on the BBC's website. A lot of the news revolved around the War On Terror and whether the July seventh attacks had been a result of our occupation of Iraq and Afghanistan. I personally didn't give a flying fuck about Iraq, Afghanistan or any of those goddamn places. All that mattered to me now was my sanity and my hairline. The two had become inseparably intertwined to me, without my hair there could be no sanity.

One article unrelated to the War on Terror did catch my attention however, it related to the importing of cigarettes from countries in the European Union.

The European Court of Justice has given its judgement on a case that could have changed the way Europeans buy alcohol and cigarettes.

The case raised the question whether someone who buys alcohol or tobacco from another country, and arranges for it to be delivered to the door, could avoid paying excise duty in his or her home country.

The court said No, to avoid paying the duty, the goods must be transported personally by the buyer.

Why was the judgement important?

If the answer had been Yes, EU citizens would have been able to order goods from a member state where duties are low - saving themselves money that would otherwise have gone to the taxman.

Since the answer is No, they will continue having to travel themselves to the country where they want to buy the goods - or pay the duty.

CIGARETTES

Cigarette prices vary enormously from one member state to another, from 38.5 euros (£26) in the UK for 100 cigarettes in the most popular price category to 3.2 euros (£2.20) in Latvia. This is only partly connected with the taxes and duties charged, which range from 80% of the total cost in France, to 56% in Lithuania.

  Of course, why hadn't I thought of that? Tobacco smuggling was a semi legitimate profession nowadays. With the addition of all those Eastern European countries to the EU, you could bring back as many cigarettes as you liked, not to mention all that cheap vodka. If cigarettes cost ten times more here than they did in Latvia I could quite easily bring back two grand's worth and flog them at three quid a pack in the UK. There were plenty of dodgy corner shops and bars that would gladly take them off my hands at those prices. Once the hire of a van, fuel and ferry charges were thrown in I could still expect to double my money and restock my drinks cabinet at the same time. What's more it wasn't a six month plan, I could be there and back by next week. If I gave myself a couple more weeks to sell them on, that meant I could be in New York having the hair grafts within a month.

The excitement that accompanied this ingenious plan was beginning to counter act the booze and the adrenaline surge that came with it felt a lot like the start of another panic attack. Breathe, I told myself, just breathe. I chugged another bottle of cider to calm myself down and grabbed a pen and paper, which I scribbled the outline of the idea upon so that I wouldn't forget it when I woke up, hungover, the next morning.

...

The reminder wasn't necessary. I was far too excited by this idea to sleep so I spent the entire night surfing the internet looking for cheap van hire. I eventually found one that was big enough to accommodate two thousand boxes of cigarettes *and* was eligible to be driven overseas. At two hundred quid for the week it was a bit steep, but included insurance for countries such as Latvia and Lithuania which most of the hire companies didn't seem too keen to provide.

I purchased an open return on the P&O ferry from Dover to Calais, which did not restrict me to a certain crossing on the way back. Once again, this cost a little more than I wanted to pay but as I didn't know how long the journey would take I figured it was extra money well spent. I then used the AA Route Finder to estimate the distance between Vilnius and Leeds, which it informed me was just under one thousand five hundred. Taking wrong turns and other fuck ups into consideration this meant I should expect to pay about two hundred pounds in diesel, I should easily double my money.

When I had everything I needed for the Latvia trip booked I opened up the website for the hair transplant clinic in New York and also the one for British Airways. BA were offering return flights to New York, which had to be booked one month in advance for three hundred and twenty pounds, which considering the time of year seemed to be pretty reasonable. I compared a few American Airlines and came back with similar prices. My only dilemma now was whether to book the tickets now and have less money with which to buy cigarettes in Lithuania, or to wait until I returned and spend an extra week living my life as a slap-head. I would have to wait an extra week, there was no doubt about it. I needed to bring back as many cigarettes as possible. All I had to do now was get myself a travelling companion, someone who could share the driving. It might be difficult to find someone at such short notice though, I mused. Someone who could be relied upon to not be working tomorrow morning. A man with no job.

I made the call an hour later.

'Good morning Dr Rossi, it's Hisky, how you doing?'

'Alright Hisky, I'm fine. How about you?'

'Not too good actually, I've been engaged in a titanic battle with the heebie jeebies this last week.'

'Oh dear, the old foe returned has it?'

'With a fucking vengeance mate, with a fucking vengeance.'
'You been to see the doctor?'
'No, I'm just self medicating with cider at the moment.'
'Cold baths too?'
'Works every time.'
'I should know.'
'Well you taught me that trick.'
'So what's brought this on? You stressed at work or something?'
'No, I just had a bit of an episode on the bus the other day.'
'What the hell were you doing on the poverty wagon? Don't you realise that public transport is the paranoiac's worst enemy? Did I not teach you anything? Avoid public transport, especially the fucking bus. The enforced immobility, the cramped seats, the ever present danger of being attacked by some psycho passenger. Please tell me you were not using it at night time?'

Jesus, Rossi was even worse than I was.

'No, it wasn't night time it was morning. It should have been fine, it was just full of school kids.'
'School kids! My God, they're the worst passengers. Don't you remember what it used to be like riding the bus to school?'
'Yes.'
'Just thinking about what Boydie used to do to us on that bus still gives me the shivers...'
'Look do we have to talk about Boydie?'
'...I mean that time that he forced you to take your trousers off and then threw them out of the window while the bus was movi...'
'Rossi! Can we change the subject please? I think I've learnt my lesson with regards to the fucking bus OK?'

'OK, calm down.'
'I was calm until you started torturing me with memories from high school.'
'Sorry, what do I owe the pleasure of your call to anyway?'
'I was just wondering if you wanted to go on holiday for a week.'
'Where?'
'Lithuania.'
'Lithuania? When?'
'Tomorrow.'
'Tomorrow? I can't afford to pay for a flight tomorrow, let alone accommodation.'
'You won't have to. I am hiring a van and driving there.'
'Driving to Lithuania? How long is that gonna take?'
'I don't know, about two or three days each way.'
'And what about accommodation? Are you going to pay for that too?'
'Well I was actually planning to sleep in the back of the van. I'm not made of money you know.'
'Where will we bathe?'
'Since when have you been bothered about bathing?'
'I don't mean to keep clean; I mean in case of an attack of the heebie jeebies.'
'We'll just have to stay calm, maybe take it in turns with the driving. If one of us feels panicky the other can take the wheel while they calm down with a drink or two.'
'I don't know, I have a bit of course work that I am behind with at the moment. What's in Lithuania anyway?'
'Cheap cigarettes, booze, probably prescription drugs too.'
'Cheap drugs?'
'Real cheap, they're almost giving the stuff away. I bet you could make a tidy profit selling Viagra on camp.'

'How am I going to get over to Leeds?'
'I'll come and pick you up.'
'What time is the ferry?'
'They go every hour until seven o' clock; I reckon it'll take about six hours to get to Dover from your place.'
'Pick me up at nine o' clock tomorrow morning. Is that too early?'
'No that's fine, I'll be there at nine.'

Chapter 28

When I awoke the next morning I headed straight to the bathroom. Not to pee or take a shit, you understand, but to check on the state of my follicular health. It was worse than ever, the shedding was in full swing, in fact the only thing stopping me looking like Kojak now was the raging acne that had begun to take over my face. I couldn't understand it; I hadn't suffered from acne for about ten years, why had it returned now? Perhaps it was the fucking Propecia, that shit was screwing with my hormones, repressing the amount of testosterone that was being produced in my body. Yes, that must be it. My body was being fooled into thinking I was a teenager or something.

I resolved to get off the Propecia with immediate effect. What was the point in growing a few vellous hairs if I was to be visited by this second cruel pox? Then of course there was the continued impotence as well. There had certainly been no improvement in that area and, quite frankly, masturbation was one of the few pleasures I would have left in life now that Rebecca had witnessed me for the disfigured freak that I was. Besides, I wouldn't need any of these fucking potions now that I was about to be able to afford my transplants.

Salvation was only a road trip to Lithuania away.

I picked up the van at seven thirty and was on the motorway to Manchester by quarter to eight. Traffic was heavier than I had anticipated and I cursed myself for not getting up earlier. I wasn't particularly bothered about being late to pick Rossi up but when the motorway was real busy like this I felt claustrophobic, penned in. I took deep breaths to steady my nerves and stuck to sixty miles an hour on the inside lane, flinching each time a truck overtook me.

'Calm down, take it easy,' I told myself as I dried my palms on the leg of my pants. But it was no good; I was terrified of the sheer volume of wagons that were surrounding me. I had one in front, another perilously close to my rear and several overtaking me on my right.

I watched the huge wheel of one truck as it passed me and struggled to fight the impulse to turn into it. I'd had these compulsions before, usually when I was at the top of a cliff or high building and I got a strange desire to throw myself off the edge. I had actually insisted on being tested for Tourette's syndrome at one point. The doctor had laughed and told me it was just vertigo.

So how did the cunt explain this then? Having an urge to drive under the wheels of an articulated lorry didn't sound much like vertigo to me. Jesus I had to calm down, breathe goddamn it breathe.

…

'Where the fuck have you been?' Rossi scowled when he finally answered his door.

'I had an attack…on the motorway…I needed to get off it and wait until the traffic calmed down.'

'So why the hell didn't you call me?'

'Sorry mate.'

'Sorry? What sort of start is this? You can't even drive to Manchester without freaking out? How are we supposed to get all the way to Lithuania?'

'I'll take some tranquillisers.'

'And drive? Fuck that. I'm not getting in a van with someone who's driving out of his skull on tranquillisers.'

'OK, then we'll drive through the night, when there's less traffic on the road. That way we can sleep in the sun instead of in the back of the van.'

'So you don't want to set off to Dover until tonight?'

'Either that or you can drive us to Dover while I get a few beers and a sleeping tablet down my neck and then we can chill in France tomorrow daytime, maybe do a bit of sightseeing before setting off during the night.'

'I've got a better idea,' he announced. 'How about I drive during the daytimes, while you have a couple of sleeping tablets and then you can drive on the nights after you wake up and I'll sleep. That way we get there in half the time.'

'Brilliant Doctor Rossi. You sir are a genius.'

'There better be a stereo in that van as I doubt I'll get much conversation out of you in the next couple of days.'

'Don't worry, there is.'

I could never understand why it was that certain things, like driving on motorways, didn't seem to bother Rossi. He was typically far more jumpy than I was and had once even spent a short period of time in the local mental hospital suffering a nervous breakdown. But I didn't want to ask him now. Once he began talking about anxiety attacks I usually felt myself getting an attack myself. His detailed descriptions of the symptoms were usually so graphic, so real I would start to feel the blood pumping faster round my own body. It was a taboo subject and I made sure he knew it.

'How's the Propecia working for you?' he asked as he gunned the van down the motorway.

'I quit this morning,' I replied taking a slug of the cider I had insisted on picking up from the shop on his campus.

'Why?'

'I was experiencing side effects.'

'Which ones?'

'A pronounced softening of the penis.'

'Shit.'

'Yes, real shit. I think I'm gonna lay off the Minox as well, I'm starting to shed pretty badly.'

'Let's have a look.'

'No point, I received a fresh batch of Toppik yesterday morning. So you wouldn't see what it *really* looks like anyway.'

'What's Toppik?'

'It's basically micro fibres of hair, that you shake onto your head to fill out any thin areas.'

'What like the shavings you get from your electric razor?'

'Yes, I guess they are. Huh, I never thought about it that way. Maybe I could've saved myself a few quid there and let's face it at least the hair would've been the exact colour.'

'It's strange isn't it, what lengths men will go to in order to cover up something like baldness? I mean let's face it, at some point in the future you may well be shaking the waste from your Gillette Ultra-shave onto the back of your head and holding it there with hair spray. Do you not think that the bald look is a little more desirable than that?'

'No, not really. What I do find strange is that society mocks men for trying to hide their baldness. I mean it is commonly accepted that baldness is unattractive yet every single method of concealment is viewed with amusement. Wigs, hair systems, comb-overs and hair transplants are all universally ridiculed. Yet it's perfectly acceptable for women to cover blemishes with makeup or have breast enlargements, tummy tucks or facelifts. As soon as it's a man wearing a toupee it becomes a big fucking joke. In fact, when I think about it, men are usually derided for having facelifts too. Why? Why can women have unwanted conditions surgically removed or cosmetically masked up but we can't? It's not fucking fair mate, it's not fair at all.'

'I guess you're right, but I think the difference is that insecurity in a woman is not thought to be an unappealing trait. In fact it is something that we, as men, find attractive. We want to protect them and reassure them because it makes us feel strong and needed. Women on the other hand find insecurities in men unattractive; they look for strength and confidence. It's a primitive instinct, from when we were hunters. Hiding one's bald head shows a lack of self-confidence and there's nothing a woman finds less attractive than a man who cannot hold his head up high.'

'It's a bit hard to hold your head up high when it's got no fucking hair on it pal, believe me.'

'That's bullshit. There are plenty of men out there who are bald and confident and I'm not just talking about film stars either. You look at a lot of high rollers in the city and plenty of those guys are bald and confident. Let's face it they are probably driving a Porsche and shagging some busty goddess too.'

'Yeah cos they've got money.'

'True but how have they got money? From a lot of hard work and the *confidence* to make it in business. Confidence breeds success my friend and unfortunately that's what you and I are lacking. It's not your hairline that's stopping you from being a success, it's your lack of confidence. Your problems are all psychological and by covering up your bald patch you'll only be plastering over your real issues. Until you address those you'll always find something about yourself to be unhappy with.'

Chapter 29

We were somewhere around Dartford, on the edge of the M25, when the drugs began to take hold. I remember noticing that Rossi's rhetoric was becoming more and more slurred and difficult for me to understand as I gave in to the diazepam's overpowering enticement to drift into unconsciousness.

'I think I'll go to sleep for a while,' I mumbled to him. 'Wake me up when we get to Dover.'

Rossi looked at me in dismay, I could see he was unhappy about the lack of companionship that he was going to receive on this particular road trip, but I didn't give a fuck. All I wanted was those cigarettes and to sleep. Yes sleep, that's what I wanted.

He started to say something, but I waved my hand signalling for him to keep quiet and allowed myself to glide into the sweetest kind of slumber, most like death.

...

'Your turn to drive amigo,' Rossi yelled shaking me as he did so.

'What? Are we in Dover already?'

'Dover? We left there about five hours ago.'

'So where the fuck are we?'

'Germany, we crossed the border with the Netherlands about ten minutes ago. We are at a service station on Autobahn Forty Two. Maybe you should have a coffee before we set off again, besides I'm hungry.'

'Germany, wow. Why didn't you wake me up for the ferry?'

'I tried, but you wouldn't respond. Those jellies must be pretty strong man.'

'You're not joking; I could've slept all the way to Lithuania.'

'How do you feel now?'

'Awake, but very relaxed.'

'Good, because these Germans are driving like fucking psychos. In fact you better give me a couple of those tablets.'

'You OK?'

'Not really, look at my hands.' He held them out for me to see, they were rattling like a witchdoctor's bag of bones. 'I'm out of my comfort zone on these fucking autobahns mate. Honestly I thought I was gonna flip out a few minutes ago. I don't like these roads one bit.'

'Easy mate, easy. Take a couple of these and have a drink. I'll get us as far as Poland and then you can do the last leg.'

'Nice one,' he replied struggling to open one of the cans of cider I had brought along.

'I'm going to get a coffee, do you want me to bring you a sandwich or something?'

'Yes please.'

'Any particular flavour?'

'Anything.'

I left him gulping the cider down and entered the service station. The place wasn't much different from the ones we had in the UK, just a different style of shopping music being piped through the speakers. Most of the sandwiches seemed to consist of various forms of salami and cheeses so I picked up two at random and made a coffee on the self service machine, reasoning that 'Mit Milch' meant with milk. It did. The fraulein behind the counter gave me a sexy looking smile as I placed the goods on the counter and I mimed to her that I wanted to pay with my card.

'You speak English?' she asked, playing with her pigtails.
'Yes, I am English.'
'You want pay with your card?'
'Yes please.'
She smiled again and leaned over the counter displaying a very ample cleavage as she swiped the card into the system. Jesus, was this some sort of German nymphomaniac? Was she giving me the come on here?
'Please to give me your number,' the fraulein requested. Christ she was. The bitch actually wanted my number.
'Er yeah, sure,' I said. 'Do you have a piece of paper?'
'No paper,' she replied looking puzzled.
'Oh, you want to type it into your mobile phone?'
'Mobile phone?' She looked even more confused now.
'Yes, my telephone number. Do you want me to write it down on some paper or are you going to type it into your mobile?'
'Please I don't understand. I get my boss, he speak better English.'
'No wait,' I replied, but it was too late she had already gone into the back office and I could hear the harsh tones of that most romantic of languages being exchanged in the back. Everything sounded like an order in German. God knows what they were saying but I imagined it being something like 'Talk, you swine or we have ways of making you.'
I was surprised to see when they re-emerged that the harsh sounding voice belonged not to some Gestapo agent but to a kind faced old man with grey hair and a handlebar moustache.
'Can I help you?' he asked in perfect English.
'Er, no…well yes…it's just that your assistant was asking me for my number.'

'Yes?'

'And I was trying to ask her if she wanted me to write it down or if she wanted to type it into her mobile phone.'

'Why would she do that? You simply type it straight into the card reader.'

'I'm sorry, I don't know what you are talking about.'

'Your pin number for your card. You simply type it straight into the machine to pay for your goods.'

'Oh, sorry I didn't realise that…'

'Yes, I am aware that in England you sign for things, but over here we type our pin number into the machine instead.'

'Oh I see. Sorry about the confusion.'

'That's not a problem,' he said before saying something to the fraulein in German as he went back into his office.

She just looked at me and giggled.

…

'You ready? Because we're going, now.' I asked Rossi.

'I guess so. What's wrong with you?'

'Nothing.'

'Why the big rush then?'

'There is no rush,' I snapped, looking over my shoulder at the fraulein through the windows of the service station. 'C'mon, get your shit together or we'll never get there.'

'You did pay for these things didn't you?' Rossi looked at me suspiciously.

'Of course I fucking paid for them.'

'So why are we shooting off again in such a hurry?'

'We're not shooting off, I just want to get to Poland as soon as possible. It's a lot cheaper than Germany.'

…

'Slow down, you're gonna fucking get us killed,' Rossi pleaded as I gunned the van east onto the A2 towards Hanover. 'What's wrong with you?'

'There's nothing wrong,' I replied sneering at him. I was the one in control now, the calming presence of the diazepam in my bloodstream coupled with the fact that Rossi was now more frightened than I was gave me a sense of power over him, for the time being.

Despite his foreign name and appearance, Rossi was, as he had said, well out of his comfort zone on foreign roads and I watched him twitching nervously out of the corner of my eye as I held the peddle to the floor of the van. Every time a BMW or Mercedes shot past us at a hundred and fifty miles an hour or so he sank into his seat. For my part I was doing my best to get the van to a hundred, which given my impaired reactions due to the jellies and the cider was probably a suicidal speed. But there was no room for fear while the diazepam was in my bloodstream.

About fifty miles down the A2 I was forced to break sharply due to some sort of tailback on the autobahn. Our van careered around the road a little but I managed to regain control and slowed my speed to about forty miles an hour as we edged along for a few hundred meters. Eventually we saw the cause of the tailback, it looked like a serious crash had occurred. There were about four vehicles involved and one of them had flipped onto its roof. I was fairly sure that the occupants of that particular car, an Audi A3, could not possibly have survived and the amount of police medics and fire officers on the scene reinforced this view.

'My God look at that,' Rossi muttered as we passed the A3. 'No one's getting out of that alive.'

'No probably not,' I replied craning my neck to gawp at the carnage.

'Do me a favour and don't go any faster than seventy miles an hour from now on will you?'

'Yeah, I think I might just do that,' I answered, thinking about what must go through your mind the second you realise that you are about to have a fatal crash. I shuddered and put my foot on the accelerator until we reached seventy miles an hour, then eased off keeping it at a steady speed. Besides a sensible seventy miles an hour would be better for the gas, less gas equalled more cigarettes.

Comparing our van travelling at seventy miles an hour to the rest of the traffic on a German Autobahn is like comparing a rocket to a bow and arrow. But even at these speeds Rossi was becoming increasingly twitchy. No doubt the crash had scared him even more than it had me. I tried not to let him know that I had noticed but from the corner of my eyes I could see him shifting his weight uncomfortably in the passenger seat and opening, then closing his window. I thought at one point he was going to jump out of the van.

'Pull over!!!' he screamed, all of a sudden.

'What? Here?'

'Just pull over damn you!' he shouted, grabbing for the wheel.

'OK,' I yelled, holding him away from the wheel and easing off the gas. 'I'm pulling over, just calm down.'

'I've gotta get out! I need to get out this fucking van!'

'Just chill, I'm pulling over now. Breathe.'

I pulled the van into the lay-by and Rossi jumped out and ran for the embankment where he dropped to his knees and began to vomit.

'Oh God, oh Jesus, please help me,' he sobbed into the ground.

I waited silently for him to compose himself, which took about ten full minutes, after which time he got up, marched over to the van and took a huge pull on a cider can, almost draining it in one go.
'I don't think I can carry on,' he said after wiping his mouth. 'I thought I was having a heart attack just then.'
'You'll be fine once the diazepam kicks in.'
'What you mean the diazepam? I just vomited onto the embankment you fool.'
'Have another.'
'And how long will that take to kick in? That crash scared the hell out of me mate. I'm telling you, these autobahns are fucking corpse factories. There's no way I can get back in that van.'
'Of course you can.'
'I'm telling you, I can't. I can't stop thinking about that crash. Did you see that guy's head?'
'No, what guy?'
'In the passenger seat of the A3. His head was cracked open. I could virtually see his brains.'
'Fuck.'
'Yes fuck. Then I start to realise that this fucking death machine you hired doesn't even have airbags. What were you thinking when you hired it for God's sake? I mean there are more safety features on a fucking skateboard than there are on this thing.'
'It never crossed my mind.'
'Yeah well, there's no way I'm getting back in it.'
'Why? Because of the lack of airbags?'
'Yes, because of the lack of fucking airbags you imbecile.'
'Well you can't just stay here.'
'I'd rather walk than get back in that van.'

'OK look, there was a service station about four miles back there. I'll go back there and get some beers to chill you out.'

'Look beers aren't going to stop my head being cracked open if you crash this fucking van are they?'

'No, but I might have an idea what will.'

Chapter 30

'Passports please,' a bemused looking Polish border guard said to us, moving his Kalashnikov rifle within reach of his firing arm.

I passed the passports to him and lifted the motorcycle crash helmet from my head, to show him that I was indeed the man on the picture of the passport.

'What is wrong with friend?'

'Nothing, he's just sleeping. Do you want me to take his helmet off too?'

'Yes, take helmet off friend. Need to see face and passport.'

He didn't look happy about this at all and I eyed his rifle cautiously. If I wasn't mistaken I had heard the sound of the safety being released. I knew these fucking crash helmets were a bad idea. He probably thought we were terrorists, or smugglers or something. I leaned over and yanked the crash helmet from Rossi's head. He murmured sleepily but didn't awake.

'Why wearing helmets?' the border guard asked.

'It's a long story.'

'Why wearing?' he repeated a little more forcefully this time.

'It's because there aren't any airbags in the van.'

'What is airbag?'

'Airbags. You know the bags that come from the dash when you have crash.' I flailed my arms around to imitate the airbag inflating and mimicked what a person would look like during a crash.

The guard took a step back as I did this and held his gun defensively. It occurred to me that the actions I had just mimed for an airbag inflating could also be construed as those of an explosion. Fuck me, what the hell was going on here?

'Wait here,' the guard demanded, before backing off towards the check point office.

'Rossi,' I hissed.

No answer.

'Rossi!' I repeated, shaking him as I did so.

'What?' he said, rubbing his eyes and attempting to focus on me.

'We're at the border for Poland. I had to take your helmet off. The border guard was waving his gun around asking me why we were wearing them.'

'Did you tell him there were no airbags?'

'Yes, I told him.'

'And what did he say?'

'What the fuck do you think he said? There's probably loads of cars in Poland without airbags, but you don't see them all driving around dressed like they're in the fucking Indy 500 do you?'

'…'

'No you fucking don't. I reckon this guy thinks we're fucking terrorists or armed robbers.'

'Jesus, don't say that. You'll set me off again.'

'Set you off! What about me? I'm freaking out here man. God knows what the fuck these guys do to suspected terrorists, they probably shoot them down like dogs, or cart them off to some godforsaken gulag.'

'Please stop freaking me out,' he replied. 'Oh shit here he comes now.'

This time the guard was accompanied by what looked like his sergeant or whatever the hell it is they have in Poland. They both came over to the side of the van and the sergeant began questioning us while the guard pointed his rifle at us.

'What is purpose of your visit?'

'We are on a driving holiday heading to Lithuania.'

'Open doors please,' he ordered.

I climbed out of the van and looked at the border guard. He was aiming that fucking rifle right at my chest.

'Do you mind if that guard points his gun somewhere else?' I asked the sergeant. 'It's scaring me a little.'

'Open doors please!'

I opened the rear doors of the van and the sergeant climbed inside. There was nothing inside apart from the half empty crate of cider and our sleeping bags.

'How long you stay in Poland?'

'We are just passing through, on our way to Lithuania. Maybe five hours.'

'Why you wear helmet?'

The questions were abrupt, to the point, but not particularly grilling.

'You have to understand sir, my friend and I are paranoiacs. We passed a car wreck in Germany where someone had split his skull open. It frightened us because our van doesn't have airbags, so we bought the crash helmets.'

He looked me up and down, then moved to the side of the van where Rossi was sitting. Rossi smiled feebly and the sergeant stared at him coldly.

'Passport please,' he demanded.

Rossi handed him his passport and he disappeared into the office while the guard stood with us, still aiming the rifle at our van. We waited about ten minutes and eventually the cold faced sergeant returned.

'Your papers are in order,' he scowled handing the passports back through the window.

'Thank you sir.'

'Enjoy your stay in Poland.'

'We will sir, thank you.'

I pulled the van away from the guard post and another guard opened the barrier as I did so. We sat in silence as I eased the van onto the Polish motorway, then when we were about a mile down the road I heard Rossi sniggering at the side of me.

'What?' I asked. 'You were as scared as I was.'

'I'm not laughing at you, I'm laughing at that dickhead,' he said pointing his thumb in the direction we had come from. 'Does he not realise the fucking cold war ended about fifteen years ago?'

'Your papers seem to be in order,' I replied in a dodgy Polish accent and we both doubled up laughing so much that I almost lost control of the van.

'What is purpose of visit?' Rossi replied, laughing as he replaced his helmet.

'Hey you sounded like a Polish Darth Vader when you do that.'

'Really? OK here's one,' he said affecting the Polish accent in his helmet. 'Search feelings Luke, you know it must be true. I am father.'

'Niet!' I screamed pretending to be an Eastern European Luke Skywalker. 'I will never join Dark Side.'

'Join me Luke and together we can rule Soviet Union as father and son.'

Chapter 31

'I feel a little hungry,' Rossi said to me as we approached some unpronounceable Polish border town. 'Maybe we should pull into this town and grab some breakfast.'

'Breakfast? At two thirty in the morning? Are you joking?'

'OK then, some supper.'

'Why don't we wait until we see a service station?' I asked.

'Because we are in a former fucking communist country, that's why. There can't be too many UK style service stations in this fucking place, it's not like we are on the M1.'

'There might be.'

'And there might not. It's better to pull off in a town just in case.'

'OK, I'll get off at the next stop,' I conceded, pulling into the right lane in anticipation of the next junction.

The town looked quiet, very quiet, as we crept along the road that led towards the centre. There were a few cars on the road and a number of lights on in some of the buildings we passed, but none of them appeared to be food outlets and we were yet to even pass a petrol station. Then we saw the first sign of life on the streets ahead of us.

'Look!' Rossi shouted. 'There, just in front. People on the streets. Perhaps there's some sort of club around here. Maybe there will be some sort of takeaway open.'

'Maybe,' I replied as we drew closer to the people ahead of us. There were a few men around but most of the people in front of us seemed to be female and almost all of them were scantily clad.

'Sweet Jesus, look at these girls mate. Fuck me, if a shitty little town like this has got this many hot girls then I'd love to see Warsaw. Pull over and ask this one if she knows where we can get some takeaway,' he ordered as we approached a strikingly tall blonde woman wearing a short cropped top, despite the cold night, and a mini skirt and high legged boots.

I pulled the van onto the kerb just ahead of her and began to wind down the window.

'Excuse me,' I hollered. 'Do you speak English?'

'I speak,' she replied, leaning into the van through the window.

'Excellent. My friend and I are looking to find a takeaway. Can you help us?'

'What is takeaway?'

'You know, takeaway,' I replied using my hands to mimic the actions of someone eating a burger.

'OK,' she said, looking a little confused. 'You want…how you say? Takeaway.'

'Yes, takeaway.'

'What money you have? Euros?'

'Yes we have some Euros.'

'Takeaway cost you thirty Euros each.'

'Thirty Euros? Isn't there anywhere cheaper?'

'Nowhere cheaper.' she scowled. 'This only red light district for fifty miles.'

The words took a while to hammer home, no doubt due to the diazepam coursing through my arteries, but when they did I took a good look around the outside of the van and realised that almost all the girls that were in the area were wearing similarly short skirts and high boots to this one and none of them seemed to be moving. Instead they all seemed glued to the side of the road, where they looked like nervous pensioners waiting to cross.

'There seems to be some confusion miss,' Rossi exclaimed, leaning over me. 'We are looking for a place to eat, or a service station.'

The bitch looked pissed off and stepped away from the car shaking her head.

'Can you direct us to a service station?' Rossi asked again.

No reply, she simply turned in her ridiculously high heeled boots and ignored us both.

'Just drive ahead mate,' Rossi said. 'We're bound to see something sooner or later.'

'I think I've just seen what I fancy,' I responded. 'Thirty Euros doesn't seem like a lot. What do you think she thought we wanted when we made the eating gestures?'

'I don't know. A blowjob perhaps.'

'Thirty Euros for a blowjob from her? That seems like a bargain. How much do you think a shag would cost?'

'God knows. Fifty maybe.'

'My God that's good.' I had been off the Propecia for two days now and could feel my loins re-grouping. In fact were it not for Rossi's presence in the van I would no doubt have been committing an indecent act inside the vehicle at this very minute.

'Is it?' Rossi remarked. 'I'm not an expert on Eastern European vice rates.'

'Well me neither, but how much would you spend on a first date if you were trying to get the girl into bed?'

'I don't know. Dinner. Drinks. Sixty or seventy quid I guess.'

'Exactly. Fifty Euros is about thirty five quid. That seems like fucking bargain to me.'

'It is, I guess,' he answered. 'But can we please get something to eat first? I'm hungry enough to eat the arse end out of a donkey.'

'Yeah, no problem, but when we've eaten I'm coming back here for dessert.'
'Fine. We'll come back as soon as we've eaten then.'

…

About ten minutes down the road we came upon what looked like some manner of truck stop. I say this because there were a number of trucks and bikes parked outside, not because I have ever actually been in a truck stop. We pulled into the car park, and tucked the van between two large wagons before sizing up the place from where we had parked. I had seen places like this in the movies and was half expecting a fight between a number of tattooed bikers to be taking place at that very moment.

There wasn't. In fact the place seemed reasonably respectable. Sure there were a few fat bastards with tattoos propping up a small bar but for the most part everyone seemed to be sitting down at tables drinking coke and eating their supper.

'Seems safe enough,' I noted to Rossi, who had pulled out a pair of opera type binoculars from his satchel and was gazing into the windows. 'What do you think?'

'I think I agree,' he replied folding his opera glasses away again and smiling at me. 'It does seem to be a reasonably reputable establishment.'

We climbed out of the van and walked slowly towards the truck stop. I pushed the door open wearily, still half expecting to hear Metallica or Def Leppard screeching from a jukebox, but was instead greeted by the type of ambient elevator music that was usually piped into supermarkets or airplanes before takeoff. No one even batted an eyelid as we walked into the place.

The laminated menu was limited and in Polish but we could pretty much ascertain from the pictures that were printed upon it what everything was. It was basically a number of chicken or pork dishes accompanied by what appeared to be badly photographed dumplings.

'I'll have this,' I said to the waitress pointing at one of the pork and dumpling dishes.

'And for me, this one,' Rossi added, pointing at some other variety of dumpling with chicken.

'Gertrinken?' the waitress asked, confusing us for Germans.

'Er beer?' I answered, looking at Rossi who nodded in approval. 'Two...er...zwei beer.'

The waitress nodded and pointed us in the direction of a wooden table.

'How much did you say cigarettes cost in Lithuania?' Rossi asked me as he stared over my shoulders.

'Ten quid for a sleeve of two hundred.'

'Any idea how much Zloty to the pound?'

'What's a Zloty?'

'It's the Polish currency you fool. Jesus do you even know what language they speak in this country?'

'Polish I imagine,' I replied uncertainly.

'Well done. Now all we have to do is find out how many Zloty there are to a pound.'

'Why?'

'I'll tell you why, to save ourselves an unnecessary five hundred miles each way to get to Lithuania that's why. Look over there, just behind the counter. Marlboro lights. If those things cost less than fifteen quid a pack we're just gonna get them from here instead.'

'If they cost a tenner a pack we will, but not fifteen. I need to triple my money not double it.'

'Think about it mate. Can you really handle another border guard when we get to Lithuania? It's bad enough that we have to go back past those fucking Nazis on the border with Germany again without adding two trips through the Lithuania/Poland border to the journey as well. If you really need to make more money just buy more of the cigarettes. Anyway think of what you'll save on fuel.'

'I can't afford to buy more packs.'

'Sure you can, just put them on your credit card.'

'I only have a three hundred and fifty pound limit.'

'So? That should be enough when you add it to the two thousand you have on your debit card.'

I thought about it and it did make sense. There wasn't much point doing an extra thousand miles for the sake of a few pounds per sleeve and he was certainly right about the border guards. Plus if we got our shopping done now there was no excuse not to turn around and head straight back to the red light district we had just passed through.

'Fair enough. How we gonna find out the exchange rate?'

'Easy. I'll text my mate Richard from university. He's always on the net, even at this time. I'll probably have a reply within a couple of minutes.'

He did and received a reply within a minute. The rate was five and a half Zloty to the pound. At seventy Zloty per sleeve that worked out at about thirteen quid. Not bad really and definitely worth abandoning the onward voyage to Lithuania for.

'Fair enough, let's do it,' I told him, thinking that soon, very soon I would once again be sporting luxurious head of hair.

Chapter 32

'Well that was an interesting way to cook pork,' I announced as we loaded the van full of Marlboro Light cigarettes. 'How were *your* dumplings anyway?'

'Rubbery, like the skin of a dead dog. I feel like I have been violated.'

'Me too, that meal was a traumatic experience. I need to take my mind off it. How do you feel about picking up a couple of those girls back at the edge of town to help us expunge the harrowing memory?'

'Do you think you'll be able to perform?' he asked.

'Of course I will, I've been off the Propecia for almost two full days now. The side effects are wearing off. Believe me I feel like a dog with two dicks.'

'Please don't mention dogs. Not for a few days anyway. Anyway I wasn't talking about the Propecia you fuckwit. I meant the fact that you have just fired down five pints of bowel bashing Polish beer.'

'Don't you worry about that mate,' I told him. 'Beer's never been a hindrance to my performance. I do feel a little light-headed though, maybe you should drive.'

'Fuck that, you're driving. I've had as many beers as you and I had just had another diazepam.'

'Fine, fair enough. I'll fucking drive.'

We finished loading up the van and I struggled to get the key into the ignition. When I eventually did so I fired the van up and aimed the fucker in the direction off the red light district. I had paid for the majority of the cigarettes on my debit card and a few dozen sleeves on my credit card. I had then withdrawn enough Polish Zloty from the ATM outside the place to cover our bar bill and about thirty minutes of fun with a couple of the Polish girls back in the red light area.

'So what do you fancy doing?' I turned and slurred to Rossi. 'Getting a girl each or sharing one?'

'Which do you think will be cheaper?'

'Jesus you're a tight fucker! I don't know, probably sharing one, though she might charge double for two guys and one of us would have to wait until the other is finished.'

'I don't mind waiting if it's a bit cheaper. Plus there's not much room in this van for four people and I'm assuming we have to drive them somewhere to fuck them.'

'You do have a point there my friend. We don't want to put one of these bitches in the back of the van while all our stuff is there. So one it is then, we'll flip for who goes first.'

'OK, I'll use an English coin. Heads or tails?'

'Tails.'

He flipped the coin, caught it on his hand and showed it to me. It was tails.

'OK I'm first in. You can stir my porridge.'

'What a lovely image sir, but it's for the best I suppose. I doubt that you would be able to get any purchase if I was to take her first.'

Ten minutes later we were in the centre of the red light area perusing the merchandise. Some of the girls were leaning over other cars, talking to potential customers, others were smoking and trying to look wanton. We drove slowly down the strip arguing over which girl was the most tempting.

'How about that one there?' I asked. 'The Latino with the curly hair.'

'No, I'm not keen on the Mediterranean type.'

'What? With your surname?'

'My name's got fuck all to do with it, I just prefer blondes.'

'Well how about that one over there? The Scandinavian looking girl in the blue mini skirt?'

'She's perfect, look at the breasts on her.'

It was true, she was perfect. A voluptuous blonde haired vixen in a blue mini skirt with matching thigh high boots. Not the sort of girl you'd want to take home, but perfect for a quick knee trembler in the back of a hired transit van.

'OK, the Scandinavian it is then. You do realise of course that she probably isn't Scandinavian?'

'Of course I fucking realise, just pull over so I can ask her how much for the two of us.'

I pulled up next to her and she threw her cigarette on the floor, stamping it out with the blue heel of her boot before leaning in and saying something we didn't understand in Polish.

'Er, do you speak English?' I asked.

'A little,' she replied using her forefinger and thumb to reiterate her answer.

'How much?' I asked, getting straight to the point.

'How much for what?'

The question threw me and I looked around outside the van just to check that we were actually in the same area as before.

'For full sex, with two men.'

'At same time or one after the other?'

I looked at Rossi, confused. I didn't know.

'One after the other,' he answered for me.

'Three hundred Zloty.'

I did the math, about fifty pounds. Not bad.

'Get in,' I told her.

She climbed in and sat on the seat next to Rossi who was wearing the most nervous smile I had ever seen. I was used to seeing him nervous, but never smiling at the same time.

'Drive down here,' she barked in a harsh Eastern European accent.

I obeyed her and followed the directions for about five minutes until we came to what looked like some sort of industrial estate.

'Pull over here,' she said, pointing at a driveway at the side of one of the warehouses. 'OK who is first?'

'I am,' I answered.

'Does other one watch? If he does, extra twenty Zloty.'

'No, no I don't watch. I'll go for a little walk, maybe take a pee,' Rossi said quickly and she opened the door to let him out.

'We do it in back of van,' she said when Rossi had gone. 'More space, more comfortable.'

'Yes that sounds like a good idea.'

I grabbed the keys from the ignition and stuck them in my pocket, then jumped out of the door and went round to the back of the van. I could feel my hard on already bulging inside my jeans. The whore came round to the back from the other side of the van and found me at the rear doors, which I already had open so that I could move the cigarettes aside to create a bit of space for us. She hesitated for awhile when she saw the piles and piles of cigarettes and I thought for a moment that she was worried that I was some sort of smuggler. But she returned to business mode in an instant, pushing me onto the edge of the van and unbuttoning my jeans. Christ this one was eager.

'You have nice dick,' she informed me as she slid my shorts over the erect glans.

'Thanks.'

'You want I give blowjob?'

'A blowjob? Will that be extra?'

'No, same price. Me like this dick.'

'Wow,' I said as she got to her knees and pulled my jeans completely off, before placing my sex starved penis into the warmth of her mouth. 'That's nice. That's really fucking nice.'

'Lie back,' she commanded, and I did so, closing my eyes as she slid me in and out of her mouth. I was vaguely aware of her rummaging around with her hands, perhaps for a condom to slide onto my erection, but I didn't really concentrate on what her hands were doing. I was far too pre-occupied with her mouth.

'You want fuck me now?' she asked after a couple of minutes.

'Yes, yes I want to fuck your little arse off.'

'Shit.'

'What?'

'I leave condoms in front of van. Give me minute to go fetch.'

'Ok,' I replied sitting up.

'You very sexy boy,' she told me pulling me up from the floor of the van and kissing me passionately. Jesus, I thought, do they normally kiss you? Or was the horny bitch genuinely attracted to me? I returned the kiss and she stood me up, naked from the waist down and played with my cock as we kissed.

'Wait here,' she whispered. 'And keep dick hard for me. Very nice dick.'

'I will,' I answered, rubbing my hard on as I watched her disappear round the passenger side of the van. I heard the sound of the passenger door opening and the van rocked for a few moments. I then heard the unmistakable sound of an engine being started. What the fuck? I thought, looking around, expecting to see another car or van in close proximity but there was nothing, only ours. Maybe Rossi had come back to the van. No, I was the one with the keys. Wait a minu…

By the time I had realised that the treacherous bitch had whipped the keys from my jeans' pocket she had already driven off, pulled over three hundred yards down the road, jumped out, closed the back doors, jumped back into the drivers seat again and made off again. But if I was a little slow in coming to terms with the situation, Rossi was positively dawdling.

'Oh shit, I thought you'd left me,' the dumb fucker panted as he ran back to where I was standing with my rapidly subsiding dick in my hands. 'Where's she gone? How long before she gets back? Was she any good?'

Chapter 33

'Please sir,' I heard the voice come from the other side of the toilet door. 'I need you to return to your seat right this instant. The plane is about to take off.'

'Just a minute,' I replied, running my wrists under the cold water taps and then breathing in and out of the paper bag.

''Hurry sir or we will miss our departure slot and the plane may be delayed.'

'I'm coming now,' I snapped, opening the door and drying my palms on my jeans. 'Sorry about that, I don't know what came over me.

I exited the toilet and drew a deep breath before focusing on my seat, three rows in front of the bathroom. Every step took enormous concentration and courage. I was on the very edge of a massive panic attack and what I really needed now was a beer and/or a sleeping tablet, but that Polish slut had driven off with those too when she had stolen our fucking van and cigarettes.

It had taken us two hours to hike back into town and find the pathetic excuse for a police station, then another hour for the fuckers to find someone that spoke English well enough for us to explain that we had been robbed at knife point by two masked men.

The translator had been incredulous, two masked men with knives robbing tourists. This was big news in this town, in fact the biggest crimes they had dealt with recently was prostitution and petty thefts by the prostitutes.

'No these were definitely men.' We had assured the concerned looking officers. 'Prostitutes? No, we didn't even realise that there was a red light district in this town.'

It had cost us about fifty pounds to stay the night in one of the town's only hotels and another twenty for a bus ticket to Warsaw Airport. Then the real body blows started raining in. Two hundred and thirty pounds each for a single ticket to London.

'Weren't there any cheaper tickets?' we'd asked.

'No. Not unless you wanted to wait seven days.'

'OK. Two tickets to London,' Rossi had sighed handing over his Visa card before turning to me. 'You better fucking pay me this back.'

'Don't worry, I will,' I replied, thanking God that thieving bitch hadn't taken his wallet too or we'd have really been fucked.

But maybe that would have been a blessing. Maybe living in this shit hole town as a tramp was the only really sensible option I had left right now. I didn't have much to go home to in Leeds, that was for sure. I'd lost Rebecca, all my savings and my job at the hotel. I would soon have to return to my soul destroying job with the council too if I wanted to continue being paid. All this and I had now lost my last hope of ever reviving my ailing hairline. In fact any savings I could muster together for the next six months or so would be squandered on repaying the debt I had incurred by embarking on this disastrous fucking trip. I might not even be able to afford my Toppik fibres, my first aid for hair loss. Christ it didn't bear thinking about, I'd go fucking mad if I did. I needed a drink to stupefy my nerves, siphon some of the trepidation and dread from my stomach.

'Could I please order a drink before take off?' I pleaded again with the air hostess.

'Sorry sir, we have to wait until we are airborne before we can serve drinks.'

'Please, just this once?'

'I'm afraid I can't sir, now please take your seat.'

'Fine, I'll take my fucking seat,' I hissed, sitting down and folding my arms to show my disapproval.
'Did you ask her if she had any sleeping tablets?' Rossi asked me when she went away.
'I've told you that I don't want to talk to you until we get back to England.'
'But what abo...'
'Ah, ah,' I warned him, placing my finger to my lips.
Rossi let out a sigh and placed his coat over his head to cover his eyes. I could hear his deep breathing from under the jacket and knew he was struggling to control his nerves too. That was why I didn't want to talk to the bastard, I knew he'd start freaking me out even more than I already was. Why hadn't that bitch just served us up a couple of cans each? Did she not feel the grave vibrations we were exuding? Was she completely without empathy? All around me I could feel negative energy, the impending sense of doom. I saw the headlines in the paper:

The stricken airliner came down somewhere over the English channel. There were one hundred and seventy four passengers on board and rescuers fear that there will be no survivors.

There were babies crying on board now as the pilot started the engines and began to check the rudders on the wings. I hated the noise those fucking rudders made, it sounded so laboured, wwhhrrrr, wwhhrrrr, like it was really struggling to move. Surely they could make those things quieter. And that fucking baby, what was the deal there? They say children have instincts that we don't, was he trying to warn us? Did waaahh, waaahhh translate to 'stop, let me off you bastards, this bird's fucking doomed'? No, just chill. Just calm down man. The baby is a good thing, that's positive karma man. If there is a God, why would he kill an innocent child? Just calm down, breathe, breathe.

'Can you fasten your seat belt sir?' The voice ripped me from my mini trance. It was a Polish flight attendant a tall man with dark hair and huge watery brown eyes. My God those eyes were watery. Was he…was he crying? Yes, I do believe he has been crying. Why? What reason could this man, this professional flight attendant have for crying? Maybe he had just split up from his girlfriend. Yes maybe that was it. Or did he know something about this flight that we didn't? Had something happened on the way here from London? A sudden decompression in the cabin perhaps. Maybe he'd had his palm read that afternoon and been warned to beware the bald man and the one who puts the jacket on his head? Yes maybe that was it. Maybe it was Rossi and I. We were the doomed ones, not the airliner. This whole fucking trip had been cursed and now we were going to bring a flight full of innocent people down with us too.

We were all going to die and the only people on the plane that realised this were me, the flight attendant and that fucking baby!

Chapter 34

'Jesus, you really freaked out back there,' my twat of a travelling companion remarked.

'Yeah, yeah, tell me something I don't know.'

'You were lucky not to get arrested man.'

'I thought I told you to tell me something I didn't know,' I snapped.

I didn't need Rossi to remind me of how ridiculous I must have looked crawling around on all fours, grabbing at the legs of the stewardess and begging for a drink, screaming that we were all going to die.

They had finally given in to my demands when some of the other passengers had begged them to just give me the goddamn drink.

'Either cuff that bastard to his seat or give him a frickin drink!' I had heard an American passenger yell at the stewardess.

And thank God they had, because I seriously believe that my next desperate move would have been for either the cockpit or the exit, either of which would have been disastrous at thirty thousand feet.

Even if the other passengers would have subdued me before I'd gotten to one of them I would have been looking at a lengthy custodial sentence, or the asylum. But thankfully they had relented and given me a drink, in fact they gave me four, free of charge, on the condition that I would sit quietly where I was and not mention crashing.

When we had landed I had half expected to find the police waiting at the other side of customs for me, but somehow I had gotten away with it. Maybe they had been waiting for me at the luggage collection carousel but as ours had all been stolen I had given them the slip.

Now, as we made our way up the M1 on the bus towards Leeds, my mind was back on business.

'Do you think the van's insurance will cover the cost of the contents as well?' I asked Rossi as we passed Sheffield.

'My God, of course,' he answered. 'I never thought about that. It should do really. Did you take travel insurance as well?'

'Why?'

'Well maybe you could claim on both, double your money.'

'Shit, I never even thought to take any travel insurance.'

'Never mind,' he said, slapping me on the shoulder. 'At least the van's insurance will cover the loss of the van and the cigarettes.'

'Yes, yes it should do,' I replied, upbeat again at the prospect of receiving a full reimbursement.

'Use my mobile if you want to call the van hire company and find out,' Rossi offered, handing me the phone with a smile.

...

'What do you mean only up to five hundred pounds?' I screamed into the mobile phone, forcing my fellow passengers on the bus to turn around and stare at me in alarm.

'I mean sir that the van's contents are only insured up to a maximum of five hundred pounds, and there is a one hundred and fifty pound excess on the policy which means that you will only be able to claim back three hundred and fifty pounds.'

'What the fucking hell was the point in me having insurance, if you only fork out five hundred pounds?'

'Well sir, for a start, it means that you will not be liable for the loss of the van, which was worth ten thousand pounds. I'm sure that's of some comfort to you sir. You will of course have to provide proof that the van was stolen. You do have evidence that you have reported it to the police?'

I hung up the phone and turned to Rossi, who had apparently gotten the thrust of the conversation.

'That's it, I'm fucked, I'm completely fucked,' I said before breaking down into tears on his shoulder.

My last gasp efforts had been denied. There would be no transplants, no Rebecca, no point in fucking living. The hair loss would only get worse unless I resumed my treatment with the Propecia and if I did that then I could wave goodbye to erections. What choice was this? I felt mentally and physically ill, I could literally feel my anxiety and depression kicking into overdrive. I couldn't even remember the last time I was truly and utterly happy in the last six months. Sure, I had fun with Rebecca but was I truly happy while I was trying desperately to hide my scalp from her? What did it matter anyway? I had lost her now too and there wasn't much hope of finding anyone else while I looked like this. Thank God I didn't have a gun on me now or I would probably have blown myself away. I'd probably take out a few hairy mother fuckers first though, starting with the fucking bus driver who looked like a member of ZZ Top.

We rode the last fifty miles on the bus in silence. Even Rossi knew that maybe it was time to just shut up and leave me to wallow in my own self pity. When the bus did arrive at Leeds I expected him to board one for Manchester and get out of my face, but he insisted on coming back to my place for a few hours.

'Why?' I had asked him, wondering what sins I had committed in a previous life to be shackled with such as persistently annoying companion.

'I'm worried about you mate,' he'd replied, immediately making me feel guilty for being so antagonistic towards him. He was a good friend really and I guess he had lost out financially from our doomed expedition as well.

Half an hour after alighting from the bus in Leeds we were back at my front door, where I struggled to get the key into the lock due to the shaking of my hands.

'Here, I'll give you a hand,' Rossi offered, taking my keys and opening the lock for me. He inched the door open, pushing aside a small pile of mail that had arrived while we were gone, then turned and looked at me with a worried look on his face.

'I'll just put the kettle on eh?'

'Cheers mate,' I replied moping into the living room and slumping onto the couch.

'Did you notice you had mail?' I heard Rossi calling from the kitchen.

I pretended not to hear him. I just picked up the remote control and flicked the TV set on. Not that I wanted to watch anything, I just needed the comforting background noise so that I didn't have to make conversation.

I had nothing left to say. Not to Rossi or anyone.

'Do you want me to open your mail for you?' Rossi asked me when he finally appeared from the kitchen holding two steaming mugs of tea.

'Whatever. It's probably just bills anyway.'

'I'll open it then.'

He put three of the letters on the coffee table and began to open a forth. It looked like an electricity bill and when he opened it he gave me the thrilling news that I now owed someone an extra two hundred pounds.

'Great, just great,' I mumbled to him. 'Any other good news? Is the gas bill here as well? No, let me guess, my rent is going up.'

'This one looks more like it,' he replied. 'It's hand written, looks like a girl's writing and there's no stamp on it. It must have been hand delivered.'

'Give me that!' I said, momentarily snapping out of my apathy.

I took the envelope from him and opened it while he got to work on another of the letters.

Hi Paul,

This might be a silly question but how are you? I've been worried about you since the other day, especially as you haven't been answering my calls.

I have been feeling so ashamed of myself for not helping you out on the bus, I was just so shocked at the way you reacted when that boy took your cap from you. You looked like you were going to kill him when you jumped out of your seat. It really scared me. But I guess he could handle himself eh?

So why haven't you been answering my calls? Is it because I didn't stand up for you? I did get off the bus and tried to come after you but you were running so fast down the street and you seemed to be ignoring me when I shouted at you to wait.

I do hope that you haven't been ignoring me because you think I won't be attracted to someone that is losing their hair, because it seriously doesn't bother me. I mean, do you really think I hadn't noticed? I don't want to make you feel any worse but it was pretty obvious you were trying to hide it: Insisting on lights being off, wearing a cap in bed etc. In fact at one point I could've sworn that you had sprinkled the contents of an electric razor onto our head. I know I once made a comment about baldness being mutilating, but I was only joking.

I just hope you will return my calls or answer your door. I miss you and really do want to see you again, preferably without a cap. Besides you know what they say about bald men being more virile and I can certainly testify to that!

Lots of love,

Rebecca xxx

Holy shit! This was unbelievable. Rebecca had known all along. What a fool she must have thought I was. How humiliating, I'd never be able to look her in the eye again.

'Oh my God, this is amazing,' Rossi yelled at the side of me.

'I know, she knew all along!'

'What?' he asked, looking at me confusedly. 'I mean this letter. Did you enter some sort of writing contest?'

'Yes why?'

'You came third in it.'

'Third! How much is the prize?' I couldn't remember what third prize was in the writing competition I had entered all those months ago. I seemed to remember that first prize was ten thousand pounds. So third must be about two or three thousand surely? Maybe I wasn't ruined after all. Maybe I could afford the implants, or at least another trip to Poland. Yes that's what I'd do, I'd get the implants and the turn up at Rebecca's with a full head of hair, ask

her what the fuck she was talking about. Bald? I don't know what you mean, I'm not bald. You must have got the wrong idea. Have a feel if you don't believe me.
 Yes that's what I'd do.
 'How much have I won?' I shouted at Rossi, reiterating my earlier question.
 'Er, it doesn't look like money,' he replied scanning the letter.
 'What? Give me that!' I snatched the letter from him and he took Rebecca's from me.

Dear Mr Hisky

Thank you for your recent submission to Rock Scorpion Press. Following our judge's selection we are pleased to inform you that your short story, No Cure For Baldness, has been awarded third prize. This means that you will be eligible to submit a full length novel or novella to Rock Scorpion Press which we will then consider for publication.

I am sure you realise that this is an exciting prospect for you and that if accepted you will receive a substantial advance on your book and generous royalties. We look forward to reading your completed manuscript.

Yours truly,

Neil Hebdon.

 'Oh my God!' Rossi howled as he read the letter from Rebecca. 'How good a day is this turning out to be? She still wants you *and* you've pretty much won a publishing contract. I didn't even know you wrote.'

'I don't usually. I just needed to get some of this shit about hair loss of my chest.'

'What's wrong with you? You seem down still. Aren't you going to call Rebecca?'

'No, not yet.'

'So when?'

'When I've finished my manuscript.'

'Why?'

'Because she's been laughing at me all along, I need to prove her wrong, show her that I am not balding.'

'But you are balding. She doesn't give a fuck, she still wants to see you. Are you mad?'

'She will see me, once I've finished the manuscript and had my transplants. Then I'll prove her wrong, show her that I am not bald.'

'What? How long will that take? Do you even have an idea for a full length novel?'

'Sure I do.'

'What?'

'This. Baldness. I'll write about my experiences struggling against baldness. I'll use a pseudonym of course, I couldn't possibly put my own name to such a book.'

I could see the incredulity in his eyes, the man had no faith. The poor fool couldn't see how it all made sense now, how all this shit had happened for a reason. But I knew. I knew why I had endured such humiliation and depression.

I knew.

But Rossi didn't. He looked at Rebecca's letter again, glanced at the one from Rock Scorpion Press and turned to me with a confused look in his eyes.

'Baldness?' he said, shaking his head. 'Who'd want to read a book about baldness?'

Paul Wojnicki

Never Mind the Redcoats

" Ich bin einn Butlinner"

'Look at these losers,' Sweeney stated. 'They get their pay on Mondays, get pissed, have a fight and, if they're not sacked the next day, they're skint again for another six days.'
It was true; we got paid (in cash) on Monday. That meant the fights, the black eyes and the Tuesday sackings. You could be fired for all manner of reasons at Butlins: Fighting, smoking pot and smuggling holidaymakers into your chalet were the favourite ways to go. I'm not entirely sure why you couldn't have guests around. Perhaps the company didn't want them to see how we were housed.

Join Whisky, one star section leader at Butlins Skegness, as he attempts to make it to the end of the season without being sacked. Not as easy as it sounds when you are busy plundering your venue's safe, fraternising with villains and smuggling large amounts of class A narcotics onto camp; not to mention making enemies with psychotic security guard, Knuckles and the very real risk of contracting a highly infectious skin disease. Will he make it to the holy grail of the Butlins season, the Club 18-30's reunion? Or will he fall victim to Knuckles, scabies, impetigo or the Skegness police?